# KILLERS & OTHERS
## STORIES
by
ROBERT POPE

"KILLERS & OTHERS"

BY

ROBERT POPE
ISBN: 978-1-716-44923-9

Copyright © Robert Pope 2020
All rights reserved.

Cover art and design by David Whitlam
www.davidwhitlam.com

Published by Dark Lane Books, 2020

# Contents

"Killers" appeared in *Alaska Quarterly Review*; "Charlotte," "The Hungers," "The Detective's Son," and "I Am Called Mystery" in *Dark Lane Anthology*; "Security System" in *Fiction International*; "Birds of Thunder" in *Two Thirds North*; "Among the Meep" in *New American Legends*; "Christmas Charm" in *Sequestrum* and *Dark Lane Anthology*; "Green's History" in *Texas Review*; "The Lost Boy" in *The Moon*; and Dragon," as "Otherwise Known as the Dragon," in *Dark Dossier*.

Look at the stars—
into the night—
so much darkness,
all that light!

# KILLERS

THE PRIZE PHOTO in the Sunday Magazine of our local paper confused me; at first, I registered only a general outline of the image and a caption: *Dog Walks Man.* I had to study the photo a moment before I understood why the skin across the back of my head tightened. I noticed the enormous dog in the photo was a Harlequin Dane a minute or two before I realized it was my own Charley. This meant that the grotesquely thin, short man in a light blue sport coat and large round glasses had to be me.

Several weeks had passed since the occasion of the photograph— it was now considerably colder in Akron—but I did remember signing a release, believing the picture would never appear anywhere. Here it was, and it startled me that I should be a subject of interest to anyone, much less the object of a prize. I think of myself not as subject but observer, more or less, of the lives of others. I tore it out of the paper and stuck it on my refrigerator with a magnet in the shape of the Ohio state flag.

One of my weaknesses is that I am charmed by interesting men, even more enchanted by an interesting woman. Resulting entanglements can lay waste to weeks, months, and leave scars on my heart and mind that never quite heal. I admit, however, I am not often terribly successful in attempts at relationships—especially when I care too quickly, as I did with Jane Carmen, the entanglement that ended with the photograph in the Sunday Magazine.

I had all but forgotten—this became painfully obvious as I looked at the picture—that one reason these attempts fail is the way I look, always something of a humiliation to me. I do manage to forget that for long periods, and I usually connect with those to whom my appearance does not at first seem to matter, for reasons of their own. Jane Carmen was a bit beautiful and a bit distracted. I had actually noticed her pacing the sidewalks of Highland Square for a couple of weeks before I actually met her. She came in behind me at a home-grown Akron coffee shop I favor because it is not part of a national chain.

I had on a light zippered jacket I bought at a summer sale and had been waiting to wear for months—yellow with an embroidered horse and rider on the breast. While the counterman made my cappuccino, I looked back at her face, which hung slack, though her brown eyes darted, looking at baked goods behind glass. She wore an attractive slate blue trench coat, belted at the waist, her hands resting lightly in the pockets. Distracted as she was, she didn't notice me right away, but when she did, she seemed taken aback. She looked in my watching eyes with a blank expression, as if waiting for an explanation, as if she said, "What?"

I blushed, looked at my shoes, but I couldn't keep from going back to the face waiting behind me with a silent, unprejudiced demand for an explanation. I hoped that I could think of something to say that would allow us to laugh and return to our lives, but I had nothing. Words I could not say erupted and died in my mouth before they became speech. In a burst of failure, I heard the shameful words in my ear before I knew I had said them: "You have a nice face."

She gave a mechanical laugh for answer and brushed her straight hair away from her face on one side. Her lips moved slightly, a gesture that—for some reason I cannot explain—went straight to my heart. I found it difficult to turn away, pay my bill and take my drink. I lowered my head and hurried out to the ding of a bell attached to the door. When I looked back through the window, she was speaking to the counterman but glanced in my direction. I was shaking as I stepped onto the sidewalk, my own voice in my mind telling me to beat a hasty retreat. I wiped my eye and found it wet. I stood my ground because I could not move. When I think how such a brief human confrontation can affect us, I have to laugh, though my laughter is forced. There she was, coming out of the coffee shop with a paper cup in her hand, like mine.

This time she didn't look at me but turned left rapidly; I had to very nearly run to catch up. She looked without surprise when I walked beside her. My mind spun to think of things to say until I gave up and told her my name, where I lived, what I was doing today, and even what church I attended. I think I wanted to calm her fears that I may have been a stalker. She listened without a word. Silence blossomed around us like something palpable. Finally, she said, "I had a son, but he died six months ago."

She kept moving without breaking stride. It took me a minute to get over the shock that she had said something like that out of the blue much less that such a thing happened. It came in a flash of understanding: if such a thing happened it was only reasonable that she could speak of nothing else until she spoke the truth that stood guard over anything she might allow herself to think, speak, or even consider. I had to hurry to keep pace.

"How did it happen?" I said.

She didn't look at me. "Hit by a car," she said, "in front of me. I let his hand go for a minute at the curb to check if I had money for an ice cream. He wanted an ice cream cone. He ran before I could grab him. A black car is all I remember, and he sped away. They never found him. I ran an ad for a month, hoping the killer would contact me."

"How old was he?"

"Five years, five months, exactly, like a formula, five times five. On the face of it, the answer, which is twenty-five, doesn't mean anything. Five to the fifth power is fifteen thousand six hundred and twenty-five. But five divided into five is one. Sometimes that makes sense to me. It gets bigger, then it's all of a sudden small again, then it disappears."

Though what she said made a kind of sense, this was the raving of a woman stuck in a moment of her recent past. Her craziness could be comprehended. I could have stopped and let her pass me by like an old shoe beside the road, but once I had heard this much, I could not bear to be another insensible object—a lamp post, a parking meter, a penny dropped on the sidewalk, too worthless to pick up.

"Would you like to sit down somewhere to drink our coffee?"

She glanced at the drink in her hand as if she had forgotten. Her purse was hooked over her other shoulder, one hand clutching it. I realized then that she had been sailing these streets in this manner for months; someone should stop her flight, talk to her, and it might as well be me.

We had covered territory in our brief exchange. We crossed the intersection at Portage Path onto the next block. Shops ended with an apartment building on our left, behind a retaining wall and a pale green lawn; the bank across the street on our right had a green area with a bench, beneath the statue of an Indian.

As she followed me across the street—a wide street with one lane in either direction—I held her elbow though she seemed capable of crossing without assistance. Once on the bench, we had the little activity of removing plastic lids and taking a sip to carry us through the first few seconds. She had foam on her upper lip, which made me wipe mine. She was staring into space, though it looked like she studied something across the street.

"I'm sorry for your awful loss," I whispered, and because I didn't know what else to do, I took another sip of my coffee.

"It's not your fault," she said.

I thought of telling her it wasn't hers either, though I intuited this would be the wrong gesture and could lead into some area for which I was unprepared.

"It's getting colder," I said to her. My ears burned with embarrassment.

"Yes," she whispered. "Winter's on the way."

It was the middle of October so we had some warmer days still coming, so I said that, though anyone who has lived here for any time at all knows how the weather goes. It seems that we always repeat these things to each other, partly to fill the time and partly to remind ourselves of where we are in the wheel of weather, so much the wheel of our fortunes.

I told her, "The *I Ching* tells us to remember that when times are bad better times are coming, and when times are good to remember that bad times are coming."

She crossed her legs at the knee and leaned back a little in the bench.

"Are they coming whether we want them or not?"

I thought about that. I did not know an answer. "Don't you want better times?"

"All I have been hoping and praying is that God would allow me to die, but he hasn't and it doesn't look like he's going to do me that favor."

I looked at the side of her face until I realized she was a complete stranger, even though I had seen her walking the streets for weeks. Like every such realization in my life, it had at least two effects: I wondered what I was doing here with her, how we came to this arrangement, and I felt shame for my inability to help her or anyone.

I had experienced this before, to be sure, perhaps not with such a burning rush, but I also experienced an anticipation of an almost sexual nature. I have a bad habit of trying to be honest about my reasons for doing what I do, but it does seem that physical attraction might be simply a factor of unavoidable biology. An atavistic part of me instinctively recognized a possibility for procreation and rose to the occasion even as a finer part recalled the commandment to love thy neighbor as thyself with a love more of fellow feeling than a sudden desire for copulation.

The rhythm of my breathing became irregular as I negotiated my various selves until I could once more become whole and human. When I looked at her this time, she was looking at me. "My name is Jane Carmen," she said.

"Frank," I said, and then I added, "Jones, but I believe I said that already."

"Frank Jones," she repeated. "That's hard to believe."

"Nevertheless," I said.

"Well, Frank," she said. She released the purse she had been clutching and extended her hand. I took it, noting the surprising

11

thinness of her fingers, a sinewy, claw-like movement in her bones, strangely intimate. For an instant I imagined naked bodies writhing in bed.

"Where are you from?" I asked. "Your voice," I explained.

"My family lives mostly in Texas, where I grew up."

"What brought you to Akron?" I kept her hand, ever more lightly.

"God, in his infinite wisdom, brought me here to kill my son. The man who did the bringing saw fit to leave, and the man who did the killing won't let me go."

I released her hand, and she stood up. "It was nice to meet you, Frank Jones."

"And you too, Jane Carmen."

"Was it?" she said.

I watched her walk away and toss her drink in a concrete trash can with a finality I felt through my body. A small sparrow, the size of my fist, just a common brown and beige sparrow, bounced close to my foot. I always keep a little seed in my pocket, so I dribbled it off the bench. Another sparrow careened to join the first, and I sat for a while to watch them. I felt sorry for the loss of Jane's son and what that must have meant to her, a thing at which I could only guess. My heart ached a little, but I don't know if we are truly able to take another's experience as our own long enough to understand that other person. This terrible event had not happened to me.

She carried this with her every minute of her life, evidently. Everyone has a story that precedes the present; at any given moment, all of the people around you carry within them their own past, their present colored by a past they will never forget, even when it is long over.

I saw an old woman on the other side of the street with a shopping bag, carrying her own distant and immediate past in the sack. I saw others across the intersection, stepping out of pasts they had once inhabited: the young bearded man walking a little black dog, the two women deep in conversation, all living in the present of a fuse burning backwards toward death.

Jane Carmen was such a person, a woman from Texas who found herself in Akron for whatever reasons, and who remained perhaps because she could not leave the place her son died, one more person moving through her life as she must. Her physical presence remained with me, a scent of apples, the way they smelled in my lunch box in elementary school, a touch of iron-tainted water, and something else a little more feral.

I wandered home without the slightest hurry. I lived another block up Market, then a turn right on Mayfield, and then halfway down the block to a small brick house I bought because I hated apartment living, the lives of others, pressing in on me from every side. Charley met me at the door with mild interest. He is a large fellow, a Harlequin Great Dane with white and black patches, as if he were a dog seen in the shadows at night. I scratched the base of his big, soft, floppy ears while he groaned.

I made my way to the kitchen to make the bacon, lettuce and tomato sandwich I had also been thinking about on my way home. Charley sat in the middle of the kitchen floor watching, as he always does when I cook. Sometimes I think that is what I like about him most, the interest he takes in whatever I do, particularly in the kitchen. He has a way of conveying wants without speech, a thing I appreciate.

What I like least about Charley is the size of his bowel movements, which I clean up with a shovel. I keep a bag of topsoil in the garage to sprinkle over spots from which I have removed one of his head-sized prizes. I don't want to go into this more than I have to, but if there was a reason, I regret getting my friend Charley, it is this alone. It is a sizable objection, but a task I have taken on for the duration—Sisyphus and his rock.

I spooned a little bacon grease on Charley's dry cereal and crumbled a piece I fried for him on top. His jaws worked like a backhoe. Once I had cleaned up the kitchen, I took him for a walk so I could enjoy the other thing I like about him: his solemn happiness, his companionship, his high, bouncing walk, huge and graceful at the same time.

That evening, after the dinner hour, Sam Darkling came by. I had his documents spread over the dining room table. He had filed an extension April fifteenth, hoping to figure out a way to avoid forking out a big chunk of cash for taxes; now, on top of that, he had the interest and fees. He'd been working at it for months and was butting up against the deadline for the extension.

I'd gotten his call two weeks earlier. One of my clients recommended me, he wouldn't say which since the client didn't want it known in town he had dealings with Darkling—or so he said. He fussed and fudged his documents another week because he didn't know how much he should reveal until he finally decided he better give me everything, let the chips fall where they may. At least that's what he said, and there was no percentage in doubting him.

Darkling had a small book store specializing in the occult and self-healing, as well as a few web sites that pulled in a surprising amount. He had self-published several books that sold well on his sites. I ordered one as soon as I agreed to take his case, *Dark Mythos,* a compilation of dubious rituals, sacraments, and myths turned out in his hair-raising style, directed toward an audience seeking the kind of spiritual guidance requiring advice contrary to common sense and medical practice.

His motto on one site was, "If it's not crazy, in a crazy world—how can it be sane?!" It had been hard for Sam to come to a tax specialist, but he was desperate. From what I could see, he made a surprising $127,000 last year, even though he tried to diminish that amount every way imaginable, a few unimaginable. There were more legal ways to diminish the total, taking everything into consideration, but he would have to pay something he didn't want to pay. Now he was paying me to tell him how much.

I hadn't enjoyed looking through anyone's papers as much for several years. The most sympathetic detail I gleaned from my perusal was that he had taken custody of a twelve-year-old autistic nephew, Maxwell Allen Darkling, when his brother Derek was incarcerated for a murder Sam argued was justified, if unwise. We had only talked on the phone when he came to drop off the pertinent documents. He filled the doorway with his frame and girth, in a yellow and brown plaid flannel shirt and blue work pants held up by a wide belt with an ornate buckle scored with arcane symbols the meaning of which I couldn't guess.

His beard was a mixture of brown and gray across the lower half of a wide, pink face; he didn't have a hair on top of his head, just a fringe of gray over his ears and the back of his neck, and his eyes were small, green, and sharp as glass. And yet, he had a delicacy of gesture almost girlish, and, to my delight, he brought his wife, a tall, slender woman in a flower print dress she must have made herself, a pile of red hair on top of her head, and a pair of the round wire-frame glasses I think of as granny glasses.

Here this man and woman had lived within a ten-mile radius of me, and I had never seen them in my wanderings. I invited them in and stuck my head out the door to see the old Chevy in the driveway with a boy inside, looking out.

"That's Maxwell," she said. "He'd prefer to stay in the car until he knows you better."

"I hope he'll come in when he's ready," I told her.

"Is it all right if Irma just curls up in that chair and reads while we hash things out?"

"Certainly, but can I bring you both a cup of coffee?"

"That would be nice," she said. She slid in a chair, slipped her feet out of her clogs, and curled her legs beneath her. Her feet were red from cold, but she didn't seem to notice. I wanted badly to know what she was reading but busied myself bringing coffee and then getting Darkling settled in the biggest chair at the table, which he smothered beneath his enormous body.

Charley, who had been a passive bystander to the greeting, lay down at my feet under the table with a groan. Darkling donned a pair of black-frame glasses and watched sullenly while I explained the tax forms I had penciled in. He had many questions, and when I had finished, he examined the forms carefully with his lower lip stuck out. His wife sat immobile, absorbed in her book, which I could now see was the sequel to one I had read, about coded messages in the scriptures. After perhaps ten minutes, he sighed with resignation, loud and long.

15

"Well, Mama, I guess this is about the best we're going to do."

He pulled out a worn check book and wrote a check for the amount and another for my fee. After he signed blank forms into which I would copy the final figures, I took out three beers and we sat in the living room until it got dark. The boy stood on the porch now, at the window, in a winter coat and hat and a pair of oversized mittens, rocking back and forth.

"He'll let us know if he wants in," said Darkling's wife.

They finished the beer, and Sam shook my hand, clearly relieved. Irma had already stepped outside and put her arm around the boy's shoulder on their way to their car. I watched the family back into the street and drive away. However strange his appearance and career, Sam Darkling was not a very strange man. He had something he taught himself to do, did it, and it supported his family. I took pleasure in finishing forms and stuffing them into envelopes to go out the next day.

I put on a sweater and stood on the back porch while Charley laid his dinosaur egg, which I left for morning. I followed him to my bedroom, turned on the radio for quiet music, and read *Dark Mythos* until midnight while I scratched Charles' head, turned out my light, and closed my eyes. I wasn't so different from Sam, though I didn't have a wife and a boy to care for.

Still, mine was a fortune cookie philosophy: Keep life orderly and everything will remain in sweet balance. Of course, as soon as you say or think such a thing, you admit the presence of disorder and imbalance. I have a rich dream life, though it always seems a bit odd we lie down, ceasing physical activity, and mental activity not only continues but blossoms, multiplying into areas about which our waking life knows very little.

I like dreaming, but am often frightened by dreams in which I have mysteriously done something terrible or punishable in a court of law, though I don't remember actually having done the awful thing, only the aftermath, when I am haunted by or pursued for it.

For example, I dreamt I killed someone—someone unspecified—chopped him or her into pieces and crammed the pieces in a cubbyhole behind a little trap door right inside my own side door. I

16

did not recall having done this but when two plain-clothes detectives rang my doorbell, I knew exactly what they were after as I came down the stairs. I allowed a search—and how could I object? —with a sinking feeling of hideous guilt. I heard the younger of them say, in a normal voice from the kitchen, "Take a look at this."

When I woke, I still had the sinking feeling on my way downstairs that I had in my dream. I went right to the kitchen, to the side door, only to discover to my great relief that I have no such cubbyhole, no trap door. Relief washed over me in stages, like waves onto the shore. I stood in my kitchen reprieved but knowing the terror of having committed something horrible—all from a dream.

I am, I acknowledge, fascinated by such crimes and relish following developing stories in the papers, but I have absolutely no interest in partaking of this strange penchant for violence. I will one day go back and read about the murder for which Derek Darkling was sentenced to jail, but I repeat that I have no wish to be anything but an observer.

Perhaps this is why, the night I met Jane Carmen and had my session with Sam Darkling, I dreamed I was home watching television when I noticed the plain-clothes detectives examining my car. I went to the window. A newscaster was commenting on oil damage in the Gulf—I was confused about which Gulf—as I watched the older one get on his knees to peer under my car. I knew what they looked for: evidence of a hit-skip killing of a five-year-old boy on Market Street, in front of my favorite coffee shop—by the way, not where the original accident happened.

Again, I did not have an actual memory of the event, but I had an awful guilt for what happened, the blood of the boy on my hands and head. I felt sorrow for the boy—in the dream his name was Tommy—and for the mother who had suffered a loss the dimensions of which I could only guess. I woke in the dark, heart palpitating in panic mode. I had to stop myself from going outside to examine the undercarriage of my car. I got up, drank a glass of water, Charles at my hip, and stood leaning on the sink until I convinced myself that I had not killed Tommy Carmen, if that was his name.

As panic subsided, it was replaced with a conviction that I must find the woman and speak to her as soon as possible. I checked the clock—6:12—and knew there would be no going back to bed. I let Charles out for a lengthy urination and cleaned up last night's offering. I showered, dressed for Mass, put on a pot of coffee. As I stepped on the porch for the paper, Charles at my side, a chill indicated winter would in fact arrive on time. I sat at the table—scooting aside the Darkling documents—and read the paper before I left for church; I planned a private prayer for mother and boy.

I set my gray hat and the Darkling book on the passenger seat and drove to St. Hillary's early, so I could sit in the sanctuary and watch it fill with an assortment of people of all ages and all manner of dress. Just before Mass began, I saw Jane slip in the back, into a glassed-in section for parents with young children. Dressed as she had been yesterday, complete with trench coat, she repeatedly brought a tissue to her nose.

I certainly never expected to see her there, but I might not have noticed if she had come in previous weeks because she slipped out a few minutes before the end of the service. Since I sat at the end of the row, I felt comfortable sneaking out after her, head down, hat in hand. She was leaning into her odd walk down the sidewalk when I called her name. She did not hear the first time, so I raised my hat and came after her.

"Jane," I called, "Jane Carmen."

She stopped and looked around blindly, until her eyes fixed on mine.

"Frank Jones," she said. "What are you doing here?"

"I'm here every Sunday morning. Didn't I mention this yesterday?"

"I don't remember. And I did not take you for a religious man."

"This is it, every Sunday. It's a habit I can't shake." I laughed, though she didn't change her expression at all.

"Sometimes," I told her, "I go to St. Bernard's downtown for Spanish Mass at 6:00."

"Do you speak Spanish?"

18

"A little bit," I said, "a very little bit. But I like not understanding what I'm hearing."

"Does that happen often?"

"Often enough," I laughed again. "Listen, may I offer you a ride home."

She stood watching me too closely, and a little angrily, I thought.

"Unless you have something else to do," I said.

"No. I'll take a ride with you, Mr. Jones."

"I'm very pleased, Miss Carmen."

I set my hat on my head, walked across the grass, and escorted her into the parking lot.

"I'm glad I ran into you," I said as I opened the passenger door. "I've thought about our meeting yesterday."

She looked up at me with that dead-eye look, and I shut the door. It was odd sliding behind the steering wheel with her in the passenger seat. I had not ridden with a woman in the passenger seat for a while. It disturbed me how much it moved me. Jane held Darkling's book on her lap, staring out the window. Odd driving with my hat on, but where could I set it?

Anyone passing might have taken us for a married couple.

"What is this book?" she asked me.

"It was written by one of my clients."

"What kind of clients do you have?"

"I prepare his taxes."

"His name is Samuel Darkling?"

"Yes."

She opened the book at the bookmark, a Darkling original, crawling with snakes and skulls. She read a chapter title. "God Creation," she said. "What is that all about?"

"It is literally about how to make a god. Or, I should say, how they have been made by cultures throughout the world."

"You mean Pagan gods."

"Yes, of course."

"How do they do it?"

"Gods are made in various ways, evidently, some less physical than others."

19

"Is he some kind of nut?"

"I would say so, but a very nice one. A little difficult to work with—believes taxes are unconstitutional."

"One of those," she said.

"He has something of a following. He puts out a magazine of the same title, circulation a little over eight thousand."

She looked at the cover. "*Dark Mythos,*" she read.

I nodded as she flipped through a few pages.

"There is an African tribe in there—whether it exists in reality, I have no idea—that makes a god for every village. A village is an extended family group, and each village creates a god of their own to reside in some fetish object. In order to create a god, they give it the name of a man or woman who has died, preferably at the hands of the villagers, and treat the fetish object in the blood and remains. He compares this with our Lord's cross. One person is designated to care for the god and speak with him and be his messenger in the world."

She told me how to get to her apartment, two streets from my house, and surprised me by the offer of a cup of coffee. The oddity of following her up the stairs to her door had its effect. I shook a little and my voice quavered when I told her I took milk in my coffee. I sat in a chair with my jacket on, my hat on my knee.

"Your apartment is nice," I told her.

She kept it well, a few modest pieces in blue and green, a glass coffee table, a patterned oriental rug. She had a faux fireplace of white brick, common in old houses in this area, once an actual or gas fireplace. Sitting on the mantel was a simple copper urn that could only have been one thing—a repository for the ashes of her son.

When she came in carrying a tray with two white cups, still wearing the trench coat, she saw me looking away from the urn. She set the tray on the coffee table and sat on the other end of the couch. "Yes, that is Travis," she said.

"His name was Travis," I said.

She nodded. "I had him cremated so he would be portable. In case I ever move back to Houston, I can take him with me."

"You grew up in Houston?"

She got up and went back to her bedroom. When she returned, she was not wearing the trench coat. She had a nice shape in a white sweater and light green pants. She carried with her a plastic zipper bag the size of a small couch cushion.

"These are the clothes he was wearing. I haven't washed them since the day."

She sat beside me, unzipped the bag, and took from inside a small, long-sleeved white pullover with a dark stain on the front. She took out the little jeans, smoothing them across her knees, then socks and tennis shoes, and little blue underpants with a cartoon character on them.

"That's Casper," she said. "He liked Casper."

I nodded.

"You see how small he was?"

"I do."

I hadn't noticed how warm it was in her apartment. We sat looking at the clothes while the coffee got cold. I began to perspire. When I finally took a sip, I spilled coffee in the saucer and set the cup on the coffee table. I told her I had another appointment with Darkling, which was a lie.

"He's the man who wrote the book?"

"The same," I said.

"I would like to meet him," she said.

"Sometime you will, then."

"I would like to read his book."

"If you come to the car, I will let you have it. I am almost finished and can get another from him if I need it."

"That would be nice."

Then, I watched her refold her son's clothes, stash them back in the plastic bag and zip it up. When she glanced at me, I realized I had covered my mouth with the fingers of one hand. I pretended to wipe something from my lips. I set my hat on my head while she took the package to her bedroom. She returned in the trench coat, and, without a word, I followed her down to my car, opened the

21

door, and leaned in to retrieve the book, very aware of her right behind me.

"He would be delighted to know you are interested."

She took the book from my hand, looked at the cover a moment, and then held it in front of her like a schoolgirl. I felt a need to say something, to acknowledge what had transpired, but couldn't think of anything. I have since reflected that when I can't think of something to say, I should just be silent. What I came up with made my ears burn. I asked if she still prayed God would allow her to die. It was her slight smile that died on her face.

I slid in behind the wheel to hide my embarrassment. I set my hat in the seat beside me and finally looked up at her. She watched me a moment, and then leaned down to the window and waited until I rolled it down. I could smell her sweet breath, feel warmth coming off of her. Her eyes looked brown and green at the same time, slightly luminous.

When she did not say anything or back away, I admit that a wild streak of hope pierced my heart and made the pulse of my throat throb. But the longer she looked in, the more her face frightened me, and I believe she could read the fear written on my face. She took her time, and then she said, her accent stronger than before, "This world is full of killers, I have learned."

I watched her face, unable to keep my eyes from betraying my nervousness, looking from one to the other of her own. Then she stood up. "Mr. Jones," she said, "I'm going to ask a favor of you now, and I hope you won't be offended."

I waited, unable to say a word until I realized she would not go on until I did.

"What is it?"

"Will you do this favor for me?"

"Yes, certainly," I whispered. My mouth had gone dry.

"Next time you see me, don't call out my name. Let me pass as if nothing ever came between us. Pretend none of this ever happened, if you can?"

I closed my eyes, nodded, and when I opened them, I watched her hair, her back, as she walked to her apartment and went inside. I was trembling when I pulled away.

I sat in the car in my driveway several minutes. I couldn't think of anything to do, until I remembered Charley. He needed a walk. It was a beautiful day, fall sun everywhere, gorgeous turning leaves dancing about me, so that's what we did.

Charley took an interest in sensory explorations; I was lost in my thoughts. On a circuit of a small triangular park that runs along Exchange, a broad-shouldered man with a wide walrus mustache leaped from behind a bush. I shouted, threw up my hands. Charley leaped up and set his paws on his chest, pushing him to the ground. When I helped him to stand up, I could see he was shaken, though Charley hadn't made a sound and now looked on with only mild interest.

He showed me the sheet of paper that had become wrinkled in his hand, and the camera hanging around his neck. I signed that release once I understood what he wanted, just as shaken by the events of my day as the photographer. But he had my picture in his camera. While I went through my daily life as always, he had, I suppose, developed and submitted it to the contest, and it won. Now it's on my refrigerator; all I have to do is look at it, to see what a foolish figure I cut that day, and every day of my life. And every so often, I have to remind myself I had nothing to do with the death of that child.

# CHARLOTTE

BINH DID NOT know if she actually heard the sound, or if it occurred entirely in her mind, but fear kept her from getting up to draw the curtains. She wore fashionably ragged blue jeans, her faded Hello Kitty t-shirt, and a scrunchy holding back her dark pony tail.

It had gotten dark as she read. The only lamp in her living room was beside her chair, and she feared that the effect from outside would be that she sat illuminated in the circle of soft white light. She had not plugged in the short string of tiny Christmas lights hanging around the neck of the white buddha beside the lamp, which would have at least provided cheer.

She plucked her phone from buddha's lap, wary of drawing attention through movement. She held it close to her eyes, finger poised over Mr. Finch's number. While she wondered if she would have the nerve, her finger throbbed, and her pulse made it twitch. His phone rang.

When no answer came, she felt more frightened than before. That sound she heard could have been nothing more than a refrigerator in the building, doing what refrigerators did when no one watched. Swishing noises, water shifting in a line. But a bang, and a crash?

No one lived in the apartment above since the old man dropped dead. All she knew of him was an unruly fringe of gray hair protruding from a dirty white visor, and a pair of enormous black-frame glasses. His wife Tilly told her the visor protected him from the harmful ultra-violet waves, pointing up, which made Binh think of UFOs. At work, she asked Vanessa, who touched her nose. "Skin cancer, baby, from the sun."

She liked the old man's wife though she never called Binh by her own name. At first, she called her Beth, Faith, then Charity, until she landed on Charlotte, asking about her teaching, and if the children today had any manners. Binh corrected her a few times, even once chanting, "B my name is Binh, and I work in a bank." Tilly always brought cookies and oddly thoughtful gifts wrapped in the same faded violet tissue. She tapped softly, calling, "Charlotte?"

She always had some pleasantry and never forgot to inquire about Binh's non-existent classroom. No other neighbor showed her such kindness. Binh leaned out to watch her laborious climb back up the stairs to her own apartment, following the pink spot in the midst of her tufts of white hair. But shortly after the old man died, she too left, helped out by unknown people, a man and woman in trench coats holding to her elbows as she called, "Help me, Charlotte."

The man who held one arm demanded to know what Binh wanted, and the woman on her other elbow glared through cat-eye glasses with sparkles in the corners. The chain of white faux pearls around her neck kept her glasses from tumbling to the floor. The woman offered Binh the smile of long-suffering, and said through her teeth. "Please, remove yourself."

Why were they staring? She went back in her apartment to watch them pass through the landing and down the stairs, with Tilly struggling between them. That disturbed Binh though she supposed they knew what they were doing.

She wished someone would say what happened to Tilly, but they didn't have any reason to notify her. She never heard anyone in the apartment across the hall, though she had seen a man in a suit and hat leaving early in the mornings. She did hear a young couple below having a party once, and smelled marijuana through the vent. When the landlord raised the rent ten dollars, they came onto her floor, getting signatures to protest the increase.

She kept quiet when they knocked on her door, until they went upstairs, where they found the old man on the living room floor and called police. She opened her door to watch paramedics tromp upstairs to load him on a litter and carry him to the ambulance in a sack with a big zipper. When she heard Tilly call "Charlotte," she closed her door and waited there in silence with her forehead pressed against the jamb.

Binh jumped when her ring tone burst in her dark apartment. She clicked on and heard Finch say, "You called?" She adjusted her position in the chair, already a little more comfortable with his voice in her ear.

"I heard a strange sound. Will you talk to me while I check?"

"Where are you?"

"In a big chair in my living room. I was reading, it got dark. I can't see anything."

"What kind of sounds?"

"Gurgling, swishing. Maybe a crash."

"Could it be a mouse or a bat?"

"A bat?"

"I once had a bat in my apartment."

"What did you do?"

"I left windows open to let it fly out. Pulled my knit cap over my head, put on a jacket, and stood waiting with the broom. I heard they could get tangled in your hair."

"Tangled in your hair?"

"It flew around the room a few times and went out a window."

"Now I'm afraid to look at all."

"You don't have any windows open, do you?"

"It's freezing outside, Mr. Finch."

"Do you want to look? I'll hang on."

"I'm too afraid now. Can you talk to me for a minute?"

"Why don't I come over and check?"

"Would you?"

"Of course."

"I'll sit in my chair until you get here."

When Finch got off, she tried to read again. Finally, she sat staring at the door, though she screamed when the knock came. She ran to the door and whispered, "Mr. Finch?"

She opened the door a crack. He had on a black hooded sweat shirt and pulled the hood off his head so she could see him, his face rosy from the cold. She opened the door wide so he could come inside.

"Let's take a look." He had a baseball bat in one hand. She followed him in the kitchen, where he snapped on a light. He led her down her hall, poking his head in the bathroom before he flipped on the light and threw the shower curtain back. He nudged a wet washcloth lying in the tub with his bat.

She held his arm as he went back to her bedroom, where he turned on the overhead. She saw her lacy bra hanging on the top of her closet door as he opened it. He stuck his head among her clothes. The bra fell on the floor behind him. He dropped on his knees to check under her bed, then stood with the head of his bat on his free hand. "Anywhere else?"

"Could you close the curtains? The front window?"

He led her back in the living room, where he closed the front curtains, then back through the dining area, pausing before closing the curtains over the sliding doors.

"Shall we check the balcony?"

She turned on an outdoor light as he slid the door open and peered at the empty balcony. Cold air and a few flakes of snow came inside. Their faces were close, looking at each other until she became aware of the warmth of his arm against her breast and let go of him.

He closed the sliding door and locked it again, then leaned the bat against her wall and stood looking down at her eyes. "What made you call me?"

"You put your number in my phone."

"It looks like the place is clear."

She jumped when the bat slid down the wall and clattered on the floor.

"You live here alone, do you?"

"Yes."

"You don't have friends in the building?"

"The old lady who called me Charlotte, before they took her away."

"Charlotte?"

"She thought I was someone else."

"Were you?" They both laughed.

"Sometimes she called me other names, before..."

27

"They took her away?"

She nodded.

"Who took her?"

"A strange man and woman. After her husband died."

"Did you ask where they were taking her?"

"I thought they must know what they were doing."

"I'm sure they did. But what were they doing?"

She thought a moment. "Good question."

"Which apartment?"

She pointed at the ceiling.

"I haven't seen swirled ceilings in a while. They stopped doing that in the seventies."

She didn't know what to say, but she looked at the ceiling.

"Want me to have a look up there?"

"The old man died up there."

"What did he call you?"

She giggled.

"I guess my work here is done," he said.

"I guess so."

"If you ever have another problem, give me a call."

She went to the door with him. He looked at her a moment before stepping in the hall. "I am glad you called."

"Thank you for coming."

"All right. I'm going now."


Once he was gone, she wondered about the apartment upstairs. She pulled her door almost shut and climbed a few steps to look up at Tilly's. She hung on the bannister as she climbed to the landing, but the light on that floor was out, so all she saw was shadows.

She put her foot on the next step when she heard the front door of her building open. She listened close. If it was the young couple, they would stop on the first floor. The steps paused on her floor. She regretted leaving her door partially open.

She held her breath, afraid she would scream when she heard the knock on her door, one light rap. She closed her eyes and gripped the bannister.

"Binh, Is that you?"

"What?" she said.

"It's Finch."

She craned her neck to look around the landing. He pulled his hood off his head, his face in the light. He had light brown hair, almost blonde, and green eyes.

"I remembered my bat in your apartment. What are you doing?"

"Looking at the old lady's door."

He came up the stairs to her. He looked up at the shadowed door and passed by her. She watched him try Tilly's door. "Locked," he whispered. He came back to the landing and stood close. "Do you want to go back in your apartment?"

She nodded and started down with him. When she stood in her doorway again, he said, "I couldn't leave without checking on you one more time." He stood looking down at her.

"Would you like to come in, for a cup of coffee?" she said.

"How about getting out for a little bit, to shake off the cobwebs. I know a place we could get a drink and something to eat, if you're hungry. It's only nine-thirty."

"Let me put something else on." She opened the door wide for him to come inside. "Have a seat on the couch while I get ready."

He sat down and crossed his arms, looking around at her living room. "How long have you been here?"

"Since I've been working at the bank. About ten months."

"What were you reading?"

She pointed at a dog-eared paperback. "*The Shining*, by Stephen King. Vanessa told me to read it."

"Do you know her well?"

She was about to go down the hall but paused to say, "Not well."

"Have you ever seen the movie?"

She shook her head. "She said don't watch it until after I read the book."

"I have two versions of it on DVD."

"Maybe I can borrow them sometime."

She went back to her bedroom, pulling the t-shirt over her head. She tossed it on her bed and put on the bra fallen from her closet door. Then she took out her boots and sat on the edge of her bed to pull them on. She fished a white cashmere sweater from a bottom drawer of her chest of drawers. She had been thinking about Finch since he put his number in her phone. He took the phone out of her hand and put in his number.

She had almost called it several times, to see if it was really his number. When she came down the hall, she stopped to get her coat, scarf and gloves from the hall closet. When she came in the living room, he stood, setting her book on the couch. When he came to her, she thought he might grab her, but he walked to the balcony door. When he turned around, he had the bat in his hand. "What's this thing all about, the statue?"

"It's a Buddha. My mother gave it to me when I moved in, for good luck."

"Is she Buddhist?"

"My parents are Presbyterians." She laughed with one hand over her mouth.

"Then, you celebrate Christmas?"

"And how," she said. "I have to get home for Christmas Eve, for the big feast."

They stood in the hallway while she locked her door, then went downstairs, out into the cold night air. "Snowing harder," he said. He led her to his car and got her in, tossed the bat in the back seat, and started the engine, for warmth, before he wiped the snow off the windshield and back window.

When he climbed in, the car had already gotten warm. The radio played a tune she did not recognize. "Like jazz?" he asked.

"I don't know."

"Keith Jarret, *My Song*."

"Where are we going?"

"A place around the corner from my house, Sammy's. If I am not mistaken, they have music tonight."

"Is it slippery?"

"Give it an hour or two. Looks like it's serious."

The snowflakes glowed in the headlights. It looked like they were both coming down and going up at the same time. "You know, everyone at work calls me Finch, but I like friends to call me Jeb."

"O.K.," she said. "Jeb."

"You said you moved in your apartment when you started at the bank. Where were you before that?"

"Cincinnati."

"Did you grow up there?"

"I went to the University of Cincinnati. Originally from Columbus."

"What made you go to Cincinnati? With OSU right there."

"That's why I went to Cincinnati."

He laughed. "So, you came up here for the same reason."

"That was part of the attraction."

"Don't get along with your family?"

"I went back for Thanksgiving. It was nice to see them, but I need distance. A chance to live on my own. I'll go again for Christmas. How about you?"

"I was in Chicago, and they asked if I wanted to transfer. Someplace new, better pay. I bought a little house in town, emphasis on the *little*. I've been here almost two years."

Neither said anything for a while, listening to the music, until Binh said, "It looks real pretty now. I love the snow."

"You might recognize the one coming up, *Days of Wine and Roses*. He plays it a little different than you might expect. Variations on a theme."

"I watched that movie on television."

Finch nodded. "The music is classic."

"I like classic movies, black and whites."

"I can watch them. I'm more into music."

"Do you play?"

"Piano. I join a couple combos when they ask. Otherwise, it's a hobby."

"I'd love to hear you play."

He pulled in the narrow lot behind Sammy's and turned off the engine. "This place look all right to you?"

"It's fine. I've been in a couple of dives myself. When I was in school."

He dashed around the car, to open her door. "Why, thank you, sir," she said.

He shut the door behind and they went inside. Many of the tables had two or three people at them. The bar had blue light, and a couple of strings of colored lights over the mirror. In one corner of a small stage area stood a small Christmas tree with blinking colored lights and tinsel.

The bartender came over when they sat on the stools. "Hey, Jeb," she said. "Les comes on in a few minutes."

"Jasmine makes a mean martini," Finch told Binh. "If you'd have one."

She nodded. "I've had a few martinis in my life."

"Back in school," he said, and she laughed.

"We drank appletinis mostly."

"Two, Jasmine," he said, "with olives. What do you normally drink?"

She shrugged. "A glass of Chablis at home."

"Do you go out much?"

"Sometimes a couple of girls come up, or I meet them. From school."

"You must have had a good time in Cincinnati."

"I did." She laughed. "But I was ready to leave."

"Well, you can plan on going out a little more, if you're game," he said.

He pulled off his black sweat shirt and lay it on the stool beside him. Under it he had on a light blue oxford shirt with a dark blue tie. "I just came from work," he said, "when you called. I stayed late."

"Thank you for rescuing me," she said.

"I was going to wait a few more days before calling you."

"What would you have called me for?"

"I would have asked you to come here."

"Well, I'm here. What now?"

Jasmine set their drinks in front of them and said, "I've got a tab, Jeb."

"This is Binh. She works with me. Binh, Jasmine."

Jasmine leaned her elbows on the bar and said, "Look at him."

A thin, black man with close-clipped hair sat in the chair on the small stage, his drink on a tiny round table. He wore a black shirt and thin white tie, tuning a red guitar. People at tables clapped. They didn't talk much while he played.

Finch smiled at her, nodding his head to the rhythm, and she laughed, swaying in her chair. Another drink arrived. "I like these," she said, tapping her finger on the glass.

When Les took a break, Finch asked if she was ready to head out. He paid the tab, they bundled up and headed out. Cars in the lot had a layer of snow on them. She sat in the car while he cleaned it off and wondered, What now? When he climbed inside, he had snow in his hair he brushed out. "So," he said. "Are you ready to go home?"

"Are you?" she said.

"If you would like to hear me play, I feel inspired by Les."

She laughed at him. "Do you?"

"Yes, I do."

She watched him watching her. "Will this cause a problem, at work?"

"Why should it?"

"Because we'll see each other, and so will people."

"I can be professional, if you can."

"I think I can," she said.

"Well, then. Come to my bungalow. We'll have a glass of Chablis, I will play for you, and then I will take you to your little apartment, if that pleases you."

"One glass of Chablis," she said.

His small house was, in fact, close to Sammy's, within walking distance. When he opened the front door, he stepped back, bowing slightly, for her to enter.

"Umm," she said. "It smells nice."

She saw the upright piano against the wall, across from a white and blue striped couch like the material of a mattress. He went in the kitchen, then came back and set the one glass of Chablis in front of her.

33

"Aren't you having one?"

He lifted the lid of a wooden box on the table, with a fox curled up on top for a handle. Inside she saw several thin marijuana cigarettes. "Would you like? If not, I will whisk them away and swear I don't know how they got there. Have you indulged?"

"Not much."

"When you were in college."

"This is only Thursday. We both work tomorrow."

"You had to mention that." He closed the lid and went to the piano, sitting on the bench, his back to her, his head turned to the side to speak.

"This is a little tune called *Summertime*. You might have heard it before."

He waited a moment, then leaned into it, playing softly. She looked at his pictures on the walls, images of musicians, at the matching chair, back through the hallway.  No decorations for Christmas, she noticed. She closed her eyes to listen to him play.

"You wouldn't believe how I've been thinking about you," he said.

"How is that?"

"I imagined taking you to Sammy's, a movie, maybe sledding at the park. The best came when we got to know each other better, and it was summer again. We would no longer think how we met, but about where this might lead."

When he stopped playing and turned toward her, she said "That sounds nice, but I think it must be past eleven. I'd like to pretend reality faded away, but I should be going."

"It has been a wonderful evening for me." He helped her on with her coat and took the camel coat he wore to work from his closet, as well as the brown leather gloves. She had seen him come in to work like this often.

He drove her home through accumulating snow, thick on sidewalks and yards. She felt slightly blissful when they pulled in the parking lot. He walked her upstairs. She unlocked the door and he kissed her on the mouth. When she opened her eyes, he was gone.

She felt dreamy as she closed the door, but the next moment she gasped involuntarily, for there on her sofa sat Tilly, from upstairs. "Oh, Charlotte, I didn't mean to startle you," she said.

Binh couldn't find appropriate words or the breath to speak. Tilly smiled at her without blinking. "I hope you don't mind I let myself in. I've been wanting to see you ever since...you know what."

Though Binh did not know what, exactly, she did remember Tilly being escorted from the building. She moved to her reading chair without turning her back on Tilly and sat on the edge of the cushion.

"I know it's something of a surprise, but I wanted to see you before I leave. They think they're sending me God knows where, but I had this chance and took it."

Her face was too made up, her lipstick bright red, eye shadow too blue.

"Did you have a nice time, tonight, dear?"

Binh said, "How did you get in?"

"I have my ways, you should know that," Tilly said through her laughter.

"Would you like a cup of tea?"

"Tea would only go right through me, and I'm only staying a few minutes, but it is so good to see you."

"It's good to see you, too." As she said it, Binh knew this was true. "I've missed you."

"How nice of you to say!" Tilly's laughter approached shrillness. "You are always so modest. Everyone else was aloof, so involved in their own lives. Didn't have a moment for an old lady. Not even my husband, wrapped up in himself, complaining night and day. I couldn't stand it anymore."

She closed her eyes, as if remembering. When she opened them, she watched Binh with obvious pleasure. "You were a bright spot in a dark life. Did you know that?"

Binh felt her gratitude and returned it, her smile coming almost against her own will. "I looked forward to seeing you, too. No one else in the building seemed to notice I was here."

Such strange pleasure on Tilly's face. It had been so long since Binh had seen her, and she tried to show her affection without the fear she also felt, but the shiver that ran through her must have been visible. She wondered if this was a dream, and she would wake in the morning without memory of this visit.

"I came to help you any way I can. If you will tell me what you want more than any other thing in this world, I would like to help you."

"What I want?"

Binh couldn't think beyond this evening, but an image came to her mind, the gentle face of Jeb Finch. Tilly's face grew grave.

"A man is a serious wish," she said. "Not always a good one."

"I'm sorry," Binh whispered. "I didn't mean to say anything."

"Then it must have been the fondest wish of your heart. But, my dear, what if it happened that he was not what you most needed? What if this proved a mistake?"

"Tonight, I know what I want, but it is true the fondest wish of my heart may not be what I need, or even what I want. I know what you say is true."

Tilly's smile returned, with a softness that surprised Binh.

"It is my great wish," she said, "if this man is right for you, he should be yours. But, if he is not what you need or truly want, it is my fervent wish he should be removed from your path."

The next morning, when she woke on the couch, she did not remember at what point Tilly left, or if she had ever come to her apartment last night. She thought about her as she got ready for work, but she also thought about Jeb Finch. She felt both the promise of the night before and her fear of seeing him come from his glassed-in cubicle to greet customers.

She had been aware the night before of a shifting dynamic in their relationship. It would have been so pleasant to stay longer, to stay the night, but she did not know what the future held for them, if anything. She reluctantly made the decision she could live with. If his interest faded, she had made no mistake. If things changed in personal ways, the intertwining of lives, it should be more gradual, so no one was terribly hurt.

She got into coat and gloves, wrapped a scarf around her throat, leaving the apartment in time to clean snow off her car and drive slippery streets. Salt trucks had been out, street scrapers, and she arrived earlier than she expected. She took the moment to sit in the car, preparing herself to expect nothing different from any other day. When she went in to set up her station, Finch had not arrived.

When he did come in, bundled as usual in his brown fedora hat, a matching scarf, camel coat, brown leather gloves, and the narrow brief case, he smiled at her. When she glanced toward his cubicle, she liked to see him interacting with customers, as if this image now held something precious and personal.

She recognized the customers who came to make deposits, transfers, or the withdrawals they might have done from home, by phone, online, or at an automated teller. Older people who hadn't adjusted to new ways, poor folks hoping to have someone explain their financial situation clearly. Those who preferred to speak with a real human being. She wondered if her position was nothing more than the hang-over from an earlier time, and if, when the future overtook them, she would have to think of something else to do.

When a middle-aged man came in with what looked like a broken nose, wearing a faded Ohio State jacket that might have come from Goodwill or a dumpster, her attention focused on his over-red mouth, puckered eyes, and the black knit cap low on his brow. She forced a smile as he spoke harshly through gritted teeth, showing her a knife with a chipped blade.

"Could you repeat that," she said.

"Give me what's in the drawer. I can be over this counter in no time flat, and if I don't stick you, I'll get one of your customers. Make it snappy, or I'll cut you."

It took a moment to understand what was expected of her. All expression left her face.

"Yes, sir," she said, keeping her eyes down as she removed bills from her drawer. When she started counting it, he hissed, "Jesus, lady, hand it over."

This confused her, but when she understood and started to hand him the cash, Jeb Finch came up behind the man, looking directly at her face. "Can I help you with something, Binh?"

When he said that, the furious man rammed the knife into his stomach. Finch drew his mouth into a puckered circle, closing his eyes as he fell to his knees. The blade dragged across his throat. Blood ran over his hand as he clutched the open wound before he tumbled to the floor.

The man grabbed the stack from her hand, spreading some of Finch's blood on the bills and her fingers. He ran out the glass doors with the security guard after him. She heard a gunshot before she knew what happened, but the man bobbed and leaped through cars in the adjacent lot, around a long building that housed the hardware store, a sandwich shop, a jeweler, and a travel agency. She saw each shop with vivid clarity before the image blurred and darkened.

After the body of Jeb Finch was removed from the premises, and the cleaning crew started on the tile floor, Binh sat on a bench in the lobby beside Vanessa, being ministered to by a paramedic, a thick woman with her blonde hair chopped off below the ears and narrow dark brown eyes. Binh had cracked her head on the floor when she passed out. The woman asked if Vanessa would take her home, making it sound like a request. She gave her the packet of pain killers and admonished Vanessa to wake her every couple of hours tonight.

"Every hour at first. Concussions are no joke."

"Neither is getting knifed in a bank robbery," Vanessa snipped. She was miffed at having been volunteered to stay the night with Binh.

The paramedic turned to Binh and said, "Take it easy this weekend. Rest and try to keep your spirits up. That was a bad shock you got today."

Binh looked out the window. The snow had stopped, streets were clear, but half-a-foot of snow lay on the ground. "We should get going before it starts up again," Vanessa said.

When the paramedic stood, Binh took the card offered. "If you feel dizzy, or throw up, call that number."

Binh didn't mention she felt dizzy right now. She let Vanessa help her to her feet. "I'll drive your car. I can get a cab to bring me back tomorrow. Lean on me."

Binh let her put her in the passenger seat and close the door while Vanessa scraped snow off the car. Tears began rolling down her cheeks. Vanessa got in the driver's side and pulled out of the lot, glancing at Binh now and then. "You have cable, right?"

Binh nodded. She found a wrinkled tissue in her coat pocket and blew her nose. She gave necessary directions, but as they went up the stairs, the dam broke. Tears flowed as Vanessa got her situated in her big chair, took off her shoes and rubbed her feet to get them warm.

When she saw the string of lights around the Buddha's neck, she leaned over the table to plug them in. "That your Christmas tree?"

She stood looking at it a moment, shaking her head.

"Anything to drink?" Vanessa asked.

"Chablis in the fridge."

When Vanessa brought wine in tumblers, Binh said she had wine glasses.

Vanessa grunted. "We need major applications."

Vanessa sat on the couch and pulled off her boots.

"You don't have to stay. You've done enough."

"In for the duration. Might not get out the whole weekend, the way the weatherman tells it. Looks like you've got food to last. My refrigerator is tin-foil wonderland. I don't know what's in half the containers."

"Thank you," Binh said. Tears started flowing again.

"You may have hit your head harder than I thought. You sprung a leak."

Binh laughed, weakly, through her tears. "I'm sorry."

"You've got a good cry coming. Let it out."

Binh blew her nose several times, then told Vanessa, "I think I'm through now."

"Thank God!"

39

That made Binh laugh again, and she cried at the same time.

"Girl, you got your emotions all mixed up when you hit your head."

"I just keep seeing it, all over again."

Vanessa shook her head. "It's going to take a lot to get that out of my mind."

"Did you know him well?" Binh asked her.

"Too well."

"Too well?"

"We had a little thing about the time you got here."

"A little thing?"

"If you're going to repeat everything I say, I'll stop now."

"Please, go on."

"We went out a few times. One thing led to another."

"One thing led to another?"

"Is there an echo in here? Yes, and pretty soon I found out I was pregnant."

"Pregnant?"

"I'm warning you."

"What did you do?"

"He had no interest in a child, so I got rid of it. He paid for the procedure, I'll give him that much. He had no interest in me after that." Vanessa finished her wine. "I saw a liquor store down the block. We need more, I'll hoof it."

Vanessa headed into the kitchen and brought the bottle back with her. She topped off Binh's and her own and set the bottle on the floor beside the couch.

"Nice big bottle. I get it by the box." Binh could not think of anything to say. Her mind had gone blank, like a bright, white flash. "So, did he find his way into your pants?"

She shook her head. "We went out last night. He came over. We went out."

"Sammy's?"

"I thought it was nice."

"Oh, it's nice. He had a brief thing with that bartender, what's her name?"

"Jasmine?"

"I don't think it ever ended. Plays the piano there sometimes. Did he play for you?"

"He's very good."

"That's what he did in Chicago. Moonlighting, he called it. He just does it now when he feels like it, same as the bartender. No messing around last night?"

Binh shook her head. She remembered his lips on hers.

"You're lucky, girl. You should get a dog, or a cat."

By the time she finished her wine, she felt numb. "I have to pee," she said.

Vanessa got up and walked her down the hall. When she got Binh on the toilet, she gave her a hug. "Don't pay attention to me. I've been around the block a few times. I'm not like you, but I've got a heart, not just a string of lights. That's what he told me last Christmas. 'Your heart is just a string of lights. When one goes out, you lose the whole string.' That bastard," she said.

"Thank you," Binh said, but she was crying again.

Vanessa closed the door behind her. "Call me when you're ready."

"Will you do me a favor," Binh called.

"What's that?"

"Will you call me Charlotte?"

"Sure, honey. Whatever floats your boat."

# THE HUNGERS

GINGER HUTCHINS WAITED several hours for her husband to drink himself into a stupor in front of the television. She had actually been nice to him, bringing him a drink to start him off, and then another. He sprawled there now in black jeans and a white t-shirt, that stupid chain he wore hanging off the couch and looping back in his front pocket, where he kept an enormous clump of keys. His feet were bare and skinny, the big and second toes too long. One long, dark knuckled hand dragged on the carpet, the other rested right on his genitals. Every single thing about him conspired to repel her more completely. So, once he started sinking back, his eyes half closed, she started getting ready.

Back in the bedroom she slipped into her best underwear and silky slip, and over this she wore a dark blue dress she never wore, and zipped up her calf length boots. The trench coat was most practical, so she buttoned it in front and pulled a sheer blue scarf over her dark hair. She left by the kitchen door, shutting it softly behind her, taking out the cell phone in her coat pocket, punching in the numbers that she knew so well.

Her skin sang like electricity; she felt heat pumping through her flesh—I'm alive again, she whispered in the phone, meet me at the stop on Washington. Walking swiftly through the narrow streets of the development, she very nearly held her breath. Her body hummed and woke her brain. The air was cool, not cold. Now and then a leaf would drift onto the road. One yellow leaf caught against her breast and rode with her before it floated off. She never slowed, trying to diminish the sound of boot heels on pavement. She felt so strong, she didn't have to see or think—she knew the way by heart.

She turned onto a little path descending through the grass, at the back of a dead end, and picked her way down a steeper incline into the gentle curve of earth where a little of the older woods had not been cleared. She touched the trees on either side for balance as she passed and heard the sounds of insects all around. Her fear heightened the anticipation of seeing Frank again, and touching him—her face burned with the need for seeing him. She imagined the moment she would climb into his car and throw her arms around him, hear his breathing in her ear. The way he said her name could make her die and come right back to life.

She ran the last descent down to the road and walked the grassy shoulder for a while. She felt the strain of muscles when she walked, her legs and hips and arms. She wanted to run all the way to the bus stop, just to feel her body move. She counted every step to keep control. When she finally sat on the concrete bench inside a glassed-in stall, she crossed her legs and waited like a woman watching for a bus, except that it was dark. Frank told her not to call again because his wife might hear—it could be a while before he'd leave, so she should wait before she headed to the stop, but could she wait? She'd have no more than two, at the outside three hours, but that was dangerous. If he woke and found her gone, what would he do?

Just a few years earlier she would have done anything to see and be with Theo, but that time was past. She surprised herself, the lengths that she would go for this small thing, a thing she called a gift of God, being all alone with him. It scared her the next day, the next, and for a week or so she kept herself in check and lived on what she had until it all ran out. Now she felt she loved him once again; she needed him against her skin. Didn't care how long she had to sit out here on this deserted stretch of road, but how she wished he'd come right now, so she wouldn't have to think of Theo waking up inside that little house, knowing that she'd gone somewhere. He'd rage and storm until she got back home, and then she'd have to pay for what she'd done.

She watched an old white car rumble past from the left and coughed in its exhaust—the only car to move along that road since she'd come down. It slowed and stopped and made a U-turn in the road and drifted past again. She couldn't see the driver on the other side and didn't want to try too hard. As it moved on down the road she could relax and look the other way—nothing but the curving road.

She leaned and looked to her left again and saw it coming back, the old white car, and this time she clearly saw him looking back at her, with a crazy grin that shocked her through the length of her body, gripped her like the air had tightened all around. His dark hair came to a curl in front, cutting back on either side in a widow's peak. His eyes were dark, his nose was large and broken looking, a big chipped tooth in front—that face stood out in darkness, the music blaring loud just then and gone again, cruising down the road, around the curve and gone.

Her breathing shuddered in her chest before she breathed more normally—it had been a prankster, nothing more, a wolf just checking out a sheep. She released a sigh and forced her shoulders to relax. She closed her eyes but opened them again when she heard the tinny music coming back. She sat up straight, alert. The old white car came rolling back around the curve, sailing past and down the road. She wouldn't look this time, but heard the squeak of tires as he turned around and came back from the left again.

She got up and started walking fast, though her legs didn't want to move, like running in a dream, but she forced them out and back as he drifted alongside, calling out the words she couldn't bear to understand. She was running now, she didn't know how fast, but running as hard as she could, hearing laughter in her ears that rattled all around like brittle branches. She wanted to scream, cry out, but if she did she feared she might not be able to run or walk. She turned past the scrubby bush and fled up the incline, but as she crossed the tracks her ankle turned and spilled her down onto her knee. It sent the heat shooting up her leg, but she got up and hobbled a few steps before she made herself forget the pain and run again. She felt a rumble from the earth, heard a shrieking in her ears, and ran just that much harder toward the trees.

Moving through a dark land now, Paul Vickers was a thirty-seven-year-old railroad man with sandy hair and freckled skin, with a space between his teeth through which he liked to whistle. He grew up on a farm in Tennessee—greenest state in the Land of the Free—but he never dreamed of driving a big train like this through the American countryside. It was beneath him, after all. He had been the minister, a preacher-man, and those eight years had left their mark. He had led his flock through good days and bad, none as bad as that good day Minnie Hoeffel laid her little hand in his, simple as a maple leaf, and lifted up her flowered dress and showed the sweetest thighs he'd ever seen.

He'd found them wrapped around his neck on more than one occasion—so had his wife, who saw the woman's role as a scourge to any man she married, a flail to bring him unto God. For his own good, she would have said, she had proclaimed his sin like bloody gospels, to the corners of the earth—still believed the earth had corners. Loved a bit of gossip, so did everyone at Calvary Baptist, even at her own expense. He'd had no choice, had to flee or face the Deacon Hoeffel, with his arms like stovepipes and the belly like a great brass drum, and the whole blessed congregation at his back.

All after him, with his snoot full of the Bible and nothing much more, as it turned out. Uncle Ned and Grandpa Sam had both been railroad men, that's how he got in—a piece of luck, no matter how you look at it, but beneath him then and now. His face still burned to think of what he'd been, and not with shame: a beaten, angry man, that's what he'd become. Old Sam had seen him half-alive and dragged him to the meeting where he found the love of God again. He had lost it once already since that evening, might again, but there it was, a comfort and a hope. He remembered Dr. Bob whenever he rolled on through Akron, and called out thanks, which he had done before he saw the damned fool running toward the tracks in the pitch of dark, as he burst through brush and trees.

"Watch out!" he shouted, and he sounded the great horn. He winced against an impact that he didn't feel. "Well, I'll be damned," he whispered.

The fool had been too slow to wedge himself beneath the wheels, if that's what he intended. Instead, he bounced off the side, right at the front—enough to do the trick.

"You trickster, God," he shouted out his window.

Vickers shook a fist up at the wedge of moon, the nearly starless sky. One more damned thing he didn't need. Check off thou shall not kill for me, sweet Jesus!

He could see the empty mornings stretching out before him now. He caught the scent of gin and vodka on the air—such a lovely night. He wiped his mouth.

Loaf of bread, tub of margarine, large jar reduced fat peanut butter, box of Cheerios and eight bananas, two heads of lettuce, the Paul Newman Italian dressing, two boxes of dog treats—bone-shape dry, drumstick-shape moist—and a big bag of dry dog cereal, a gallon of milk, and a six pack of sixty watt soft white bulbs: that's what sat in the passenger seat of Stanley Williams' Buick Riviera as he drove past a bus stop on Washington Boulevard and slowly pulled to the curb across from a flickering street lamp.

His wife, Coleen, had left the message on his cell, which he played back while he pushed a cart through the aisles of an open all-night Giant Eagle to remind him what she wanted. He picked up these things mechanically, thinking of nothing but the rattle of ice cubes in a scotch glass when he got home, out of the suit and shoes, and put his feet up on the ottoman to watch a few minutes of the news before crawling in bed beside her. He'd already flipped the switch that turned off his brain, but it turned on automatically when he saw the old white Ford at the side of the road, its front door partly open on the street and the passenger side tires up over the curb—license plate WHO 5260.

He sat in his car, watching and listening a few minutes, engine still running. He unbuttoned his collar, pulled off his tie, laid it on the bags in the passenger seat. After a couple of minutes, he turned off his engine. The lights of the Ford, several car lengths in front of him, were dim, muted almost to nothing. Looked like the engine wasn't running, but that didn't mean it hadn't been when the driver pulled over.

He watched at least five minutes before getting out of his car. He was a forty-two-year-old African-American detective with two kids at home, sixteen-year-old Coretta and fourteen-year-old Stanley junior, who insisted on being called by his middle name, Sean, and their dependence on him always made him cautious. At the same time, being six foot four inches and weighing in at two fifty these days tended to make him bold.

He took the long flashlight from under the glove compartment and switched it on as he approached the Ford, moving into the center of the right lane as he came up beside the car. He held the flashlight beside his head and looked into the front seat and then the back. He directed the beam beyond the car, around the other side. A scrubby hedge gave way to a nearly hidden path that ran up and across the railroad tracks twenty yards ahead. A stand of trees and bushes separated the tracks from an older development, perhaps seventy yards back off the road. He'd passed the empty bus stop on Washington, not much else until you got around the curve ahead—small bars and body shops.

The breeze was pleasant. It had been a cool fall day, turning a little cooler when the sun went down. Now, this little piece of geography had risen out of his ride home, a place he wouldn't have thought about, to have a meaning he couldn't quite place yet, but something. Ahead, to his left, the trees and bushes came down to the road before they'd been cleared out further on. The tracks curved in from the west up there with the curving of the road. Moon at the half, pale, five stars visible, plus Venus—no more than normal sounds of crickets and traffic from the freeway behind.

He walked up to the car, looked inside again. Keys in the ignition and the smell of marijuana would earn this one a closer look, but he could see nothing unusual in plain view. He reached in, popped the trunk, and went around the back—spare tire, not bolted down, jack loose, couple of tools, dirty looking jacket, pair of gloves, a thermos, a roll of duct tape. He left the lid up and stepped on the curb, searching the ground.

47

He shined the beam higher, took a dozen steps up toward the tracks—something definitely unusual, a man on the ground, head toward him, arm above his head, the other tucked beside his body, legs crossed maybe. Stanley approached, cautious, searching the ground between him and the body—looked like he'd been shot in the midst of a spinning leap. The white, bloodied head looked back at him, mouth open, the gray shirt torn, blue jeans, tan work boots. He shined a light on the tracks, following the curve to where they disappeared into the trees on his left, then onto the narrow, crooked trees ahead—the few remaining leaves waved gently.

When he stood beside the body, he studied it a while, but it told him little more than what he'd already noted. He looked across the tracks, into the trees—he didn't want to go in there, but he picked up something else, scent of perfume, faint. Just then, and it was gone. He shined the light on the ground and found a narrow hole, size of a woman's heel, the heel of a boot perhaps, beyond that, a fainter impression, and then the tracks.

He walked across the tracks and crouched, looking for any sign on the other side. He stuck a finger into the next impression he found: shape of a heel, flat at the front and round at the back, an inch deep. When he stood, he saw a thin black scarf stirring in the breeze, sheer, drifting in the air. He smelled faint scent still in it, prodded deeper into the branches with his beam; shadows did a wicked, jerky dance. He sniffed the air, lumbered into the trees. An instinct told him, with a prickling at his neck, to go back to the car and call for backup, but the scarf caught in his mind as well as on the branch, the prospect of a woman in this wood ahead. He crept through the trees, smelling deeply now, listening for the slightest rustle different from the trees and insects.

When he came out the other side, he looked into a dark neighborhood, clapboard houses crouching in the night. Those narrow streets would hide her better than the trees. Someone had come this way, had run through here. He'd seen no blood, but she could be in this wood or up ahead, anywhere by now. He headed back through trees, across tracks, to stand beside the body, where he called for a patrol car and ambulance, though this one would likely need the morgue. He didn't see how anyone who looked like him could be alive, but stranger things had happened. A yellow leaf stuck to the toe of his left shoe.

The breeze felt good against his face.

Leslie Ward came down a corridor toward a waiting room where she saw the woman on her knees, three children behind her, two boys and a tired looking little red-haired girl leaning on the older one. She didn't hurry—she'd get there soon enough. How odd it still surprised her: this one was blond, with a pale complexion. She half expected darker tones and different wails of lamentation.

She had been alerted; she knew the sketch—the husband had wandered into the path of an oncoming train. They worked on him with little hope. She didn't doubt that he'd been drinking—how else would a man walk into a train? There were things she didn't understand, but then, she didn't need to know it any better than she did. She understood the pattern and what else really mattered? The human situation, she knew well enough.

Those kids would have to adjust, one way or another; they would have their grief as well, perhaps for years to come, but right now Mom pre-empted them in grief, if grief it was. She had seen the story from far off: *What have you done to me? What am I to do now?* That would be the summary. She wasn't jaded—she just knew the situation all too well: the woman on her knees, elaborating grievances, two boys and a little girl behind to illustrate her point. *My God, what have you done to me—took my husband, left me with three kids? Why not take us all and have done with it?*

When she kneeled beside the woman, she revealed none of this, of course. She clasped her hands and laid them on her thighs. "Marie? I'm the hospital chaplain. I hope that I can help you in some way." She became self-conscious of her own slacks and white lab coat—the way she always had when differences were greater. Marie had on the huge pink coat, gray sweat pants, and tennis shoes. She'd pulled her hair in a pony tail as she'd rushed to get herself and these kids dressed, for what? They'd all been roused from sleep—at least that much was clear. Marie had shriveled up the tissue in her hand wiping at her nose.

The issue could not now be how much she loved him; she had those kids to think about. The woman said she didn't know how much the insurance from his work would pay if he actually died—would they still consider him an employee? He had some life insurance from his work, how much she didn't know. It couldn't be that much the way they worked the benefits out there. Who thought she'd need it so soon?

She didn't even know what they had in the bank, hadn't paid attention, now they told her he'd been sideswiped by a train. What did that mean?

How'd he get so close? The car beside the road—had he been going for help or walking home? If he'd carried a cell phone, he could have called and she'd have said, Sit tight and I'll tell Michael. Michael was her step-Dad, who would have picked him up, if he hadn't drunk too much, or even if he had. It might have been light out if it happened a couple of weeks ago, before the daylight savings time. He would have made it home, not lay there half the night. How long did he just lay there by the tracks, sprawled like he'd passed out from drink? She hoped it wasn't drink, not with what these kids would have to deal with now—these boys you gave us, Lord, this poor fatherless girl.

Tears sparkled in her eyes. This little redhead girl you gave us just four years ago: why, if you were going to take the food out of our mouths? Sorry, kids, the Lord decided you should go without a father—your mother has to get a job and work all day. Is that what I'm to tell them, Lord? What sense will that make to kids when gas comes due in the dead of winter? Is this the way you treat your faithful servants? I'd thought better of you, Lord! I'd thought better and told these kids as much. I said, God won't let us down, you kids. He's watching over us. He's got us in the palm of his great big old hand. Didn't I say that, kids? That's what I said, and now I have to take it back. They say he's dying, looks like he'll be gone before too long because you had to hit him with a train. Well, I want him back, right now.

"God *is* watching over you, Marie," she said.

"Am I to be alone with my three babies here?" They gathered in and let her put her arms around them.

"I don't know, but I can find out more for you, if you'd like."

"Don't," she gasped. She clutched at Leslie's arm. "Just pray with us right now. Ask God to bring him back. Tell Him let my Hank come home. He needs to take care of his babies, tell Him that."

The chaplain leaned closer and seemed to hold them in her arms, all four of them, and said the very thing she never should have said: "God, you see how much this woman needs him now. What is his name?"

"It's Hank. It's William. William Henry Hunger, we live on Bloom, that's on the East. My name's Marie and this is Phil and Peter and Bet. We go to church each Sunday of the week, so He should know us."

"Dear God, you know Marie and her children, and her husband Hank."

"William Henry Hunger, say it full."

"You know him, William Henry Hunger. Watch over him and his little family."

"Not just that."

"And if it is your will, save her husband and the father of these children."

"Don't say that about His will. You're supposed to ask for things. It says remind Him, he promised He would answer to our prayers."

The chaplain closed her eyes. "You've said that you would listen to the prayers of those who kept your faith. You said that you would answer prayers. Marie is asking this of you, let her husband William Henry Hunger come back to his family, where he's desperately needed. We lay this at your feet, O Lord, in the hope that you will grant this request made in their hour of need."

"And Jesus," Marie added, "I'm asking you not to work in mysterious ways this time. I'm asking you flat out, let Hank come back. Let him come and go from our house on Bloom again, let him work and support us like he did before. Let him take care of us like he's supposed to do."

51

Leslie said, "Amen." They sat there quietly a while. "Are you all right now?"

Marie nodded and allowed the chaplain to help her into a chair, her boys on either side, that little girl between her knees. The chaplain said she'd be right back and hurried down the corridor, nearly running for a bathroom. She lunged inside, shut and locked the door with shaking hands, and hung over the toilet, clutching at the seat. A deep belch ripped out of her, and then another, and then her whole breakfast, nothing more than a bran muffin, a glass of orange juice and a cup of coffee, but there it was, in pieces and in slimy strings.

When she had nothing more to give, she stood, her mouth still open, salivating, and swung to the sink. It felt just like it had those early days in college, long ago, when she'd discovered drinking with her friends, short lived—her only thirst was for the Lord. She washed her hands and arms, her mouth and face, using half a dozen paper towels to dry herself. She stood swaying in the bathroom with her eyes closed for a while, until the dizziness began to calm. Marie had set her off—that pathetic woman worrying about her life insurance, money in the bank. Pitying herself while those three awful children stood behind with faces blank as slack-jaw idiots. Did she think they couldn't hear? Did she have an eyelash worth of love left in her heart?

She staggered to an elevator and rode down to the main floor. She went out the big glass doors, into the luminous gray daylight. Small yellow leaves rained down from little trees across the street. They jumped and swirled whenever any car drove past. The breeze was cold against her face. She wiped her cheeks.

She knew that she was wrong, shouldn't feel this way—if justice was kind, this woman and her children wouldn't have to live without her husband and their father. But God would grant a miracle or not. What she had seen would make it a sad joke—soldiers living, dying, losing limbs; hearing their confessions, questions, living with their cries for help. Iraqi families torn apart by bombs and bullets, young men and women putting up brave fronts against the tragedy to come—that's where she learned her deadly trade, this hospital no more than substitute for something she could no longer have. She had begged to be sent back and been told no. All the severed limbs still writhed together in her brain at night, the screams of pain and faces full of inescapable self-knowledge.

Nothing in this world would make her feel alive again.

Hank woke in pure darkness. When he set his feet on the floor, it seemed firm enough, so he stood. He noticed a rim of light around a door and walked to it, but where the knob ought to be he found nothing but a smooth, flat surface. He felt beside the door and found a switch, but when the light burst all around him, he began to float up until he bumped the ceiling, looking down on a bright, white room inside of which two men in surgical gowns worked on a body on a narrow bed or table. Three others gave assistance with barely any speech he could make out. The body on the table looked so beat up and bloody he couldn't see how it could be alive.

How did I end up like this, he asked himself? At that moment, he slipped through the ceiling and came through the floor of a ward immediately above surgery, where two nurses sat behind a counter. A third leaned on the other side, a file in one hand, talking in a hollow voice about her husband's search for a job. One nurse looked up with no response and looked down again. Through a curtain behind the talking nurse he glimpsed a white-haired woman, mouth wide open, stretched out under a white sheet, her tiny feet in gray socks sticking out the end.

He disappeared into the ceiling once again and came through the floor above, into a room in which a man propped up in bed was talking very seriously to another in a suit and tie. He tried to hear the words, but picked up only a few phrases about the Ohio State football game on the television above them. He was moving more rapidly—three floors passed without detail—and came out in the open air, a gray day in autumn. He saw trees shedding leaves on one side of the hospital, a highway on the other, and then it was just like it looked from an airplane, all the little houses and miniature cars moving down scale streets. Clouds came next, gray underneath, white and golden from above. He tried to slow himself, holding out his arms and legs, but disappeared inside a wet, gray cloud a while and found that he was walking through a cloudscape of shifting gray and purplish banks on either side.

He walked along until he came upon a tunnel, the sort in which a train might disappear as it passed through a hill. He strained to see what he could inside—darkness growing darker until it looked like a painted façade, a dark door into a tunnel fashioned of large gray stones, huge blocks of stone cut from an abandoned quarry like the one to which he took a young woman once upon a time, far away and long ago. He drove her there with duct tape around wrists and mouth, lying in the back seat, whimpering and crying, the music blaring. His face burned in remembering. When he went home, she stayed behind, wrists and ankles bound again, silent in the river flowing past.

He wondered now how deep inside these stones continued, but the blackness through the entrance looked like a door through which he'd have to pass to find out more. He put his head into the dark, but when he realized he could feel it, took it out again. Still, he had heard about a tunnel, and the faces he would find inside—his grandmother, his father who died of lung cancer, his younger brother John who joined the army and lost his life in Afghanistan.

The word meant nothing to him now; where was Afghanistan? He looked behind him, back in the folds of clouds. How senseless it had been, he told John so—now he hoped it would be his brother John who came to show the way. He groped along the tunnel wall, swallowed up in darkness, imagining how his brother John would look, how gladly he would find his brother now—if only he would show up soon. He was afraid to take his hands from the wall, walking sideways like a crab, arms outstretched in front of him, straining to see anything in the direction he was moving. The path on which his feet shuffled might be no wider than a narrow walkway, on the other side—he didn't know. He listened through the silence and heard only the movement of his feet, but the longer he listened the more feet he heard, the sound of movement through the darkness of the tunnel.

When he looked back, he saw another man scooting along behind him, hands moving on the wall like his and looking back, as he was. He saw almost immediately, or knew, this too was him; behind this one, how many more? He looked ahead, in the direction he was edging, and saw himself repeated there as well. He wanted to call out his brother's name, but who might be near to be alerted that he was there? What if eyes saw him in blackness as he saw in the light?

There in the distance, far ahead, a fading glow, like the headlamp of a car with a dying battery. His hands and arms and shoulders ached, his feet and ankles burned as he picked up the pace. The beating of his heart echoed through the tunnel, throbbing in the rhythm of his feet and hands until he thought he couldn't keep from screaming out—even his own breathing entered in the mayhem. Tears rolled down his cheeks. He heard a whimper and assumed it came from him.

Then it stopped and nothing once again but silence. He moved as swiftly as he could, but he lost all sense of movement in his legs and arms. The faint glow was approaching, slowly; he saw it pulsing, feared that it might disappear—yards ahead and emanating from the floor. When he stood beside it his relief was turned to grief by the simple fact that he could not see in it. He couldn't bring himself to take his hands off the wall, or slide his feet closer.

The light did not spread or suffuse but held into itself, its own illumination. He feared that he would fall if he removed his hands—they had frozen there, locked against the surface that they followed. He would have to take a chance or cling forever. He leaned out over the light, but his shoulders ached, refusing to let him look into the hole. At last, he jerked away to peer into the light, and though he tried to stop himself, he pitched from darkness into light. As he fell, he saw the body on a table once again, the doctors, nurses working on the open chest. He saw a battered face, the open mouth and broken teeth, the black tube going down the throat. He tumbled down onto the body, and then he slipped inside like it was made of quicksand, water, extending through the arms and legs. Pain

55

gripped like electricity, ripping through his mind with searing fire. He writhed and tried to scream but nothing came.

# SECURITY SYSTEM

BETTY PERCHED IN the big yellow recliner, her legs crossed beneath her, talking on her phone. She rubbed her forehead with the palm of her free hand, fingers curved back to allow her nails to dry without chipping or smearing. She held the phone with her thumb only. After a moment, she jumped out of her chair and paced the room.

"OK," she said. "He comes home 5:20. There's a ten-minute break in security, he comes in, kisses me on the cheek, goes straight to the bathroom, sits on the crapper for twenty minutes, reading the paper. You wait five minutes, 5:25, you have another five before reset." She glanced at the clock, which was clicking maniacally to catch up with itself—does this every afternoon before the security break. "J's fanatic about our security, and it'll record the time, so it can't vary. You don't get in the bedroom window between 5:25 and 5:30, it's off, understand?

"Leave the window open—it's your only way out. If you try the front door it sets off an alarm on his phone. He keeps his wad in the bottom drawer of the dresser, under old clothes he never wears. Hundreds, maybe thousands, I don't know how much. He's got some kind of trap so he knows if anyone—namely me—gets into his stash, some thread or something. Open all the drawers, quickly, toss the stuff, like you searched. The gun too. Take that, just to be safe, but don't use it. No noise until we're set.

"Listen, Karl, he's dangerous. So, get this straight, all right?" She stood in the middle of the room now, looking up at the ceiling. "Come down the hallway, through the living room. I'll be here, with headphones, doing my dancercise. My back will be to you. I'll have my eyes closed while you sneak into the kitchen, in the pantry, a tight squeeze. Your skinny butt should manage that no problem."

She listened while she paced back and forth. "No, no, just wait in there and don't make a sound. Hold your breath. When he comes in the kitchen to get his beer out of the fridge, like he always does, step out and let him have it, one quick one, right on the head. You do not want him to recover, I guarantee you. He's a real fire-breather when he feels threatened. He's got to go down, but hit him again two or three more times to make sure. I repeat, you do not want him to get up. You've got the axe, right?

"Afterwards, you come running into the living room, grab me by the hair or the neck or something, so I get blood on me, knock me down after I scream once, just enough for someone to hear but not long enough to make them come running. Knock me out, sweetie. Yes, hard, and get out the back window again. Upstairs will be home, so you don't want them to see you. Get away, two blocks down where you left your clothes, strip, throw everything in the barrel, and pour the gasoline on everything. Then the gloves. Get dressed, walk away. Leave the barrel on fire and get." She dropped onto the orange couch and closed her eyes, breathing heavily.

"We got to lay low a week or two before we see each other. I don't know how long it takes for insurance to come through. We don't want trouble with that. Once we got that, we'll be free, baby. You and me. Jim doesn't suspect a thing. He expects me to be waiting when he comes home. I get his dinner, he drinks a dozen beers, watches TV, that's it. I don't exist all day, he has no idea. Knows nothing about us, doesn't have a clue. I can't wait to actually see you."

She glanced at the clock on the wall, the hands clicking around the face. "Look at the time! I'm getting off now. He'll be home in a couple. Take care of yourself, baby. Do just like I told you, we'll be all right. If they do catch one of us, just keep quiet, no matter what they tell you. I'd never say anything about you. I'll just tell it straight, like a robbery, like I don't know who did it. If it's you they get, play dumb. That shouldn't be hard.

"You don't know what they're talking about. No matter what they say, like if they tell you I squealed. I'd never do that, baby. I'd die first."

She turned her phone off and set it on the table beside the couch. She waved her hands in the air to make sure her nails had dried and waited on the couch for J to come home. She tried to pick up a book she'd been reading, *A Swell-Looking Babe*, by Jim Thompson, but none of the words meant anything to her. All she could think about was getting out of Akron, Ohio.

K hid in hedges taller than himself, arms at his sides, hoping no one would see him sticking out on either side of the greenery. The axe shoved under his belt made him feel awkward. He would have preferred doing this in the dark, but B warned him J's security system only shut down for ten minutes when J came home from work.

A large dragonfly hovered between him and the yellow stucco wall of the building, a purple hue in its wings. He had heard of drones that could spy on you wherever you were and thought this might be one of them, disguised as a dragonfly. Maybe a camera had been attached to a real dragonfly, one that had been given some kind of injection to encourage growth.

It hung in the air, just close enough that he could have reached out and grabbed it. He heard the click he was waiting for—security system shutting down—and moved to the building, slid the window open, pulled himself up to the opening. The dragonfly followed. He paused to take a swipe at it. It backed out of reach and returned to watch him climb through the window.

When he dropped to the floor, he looked up to see the dragonfly following him inside. He waved his hand at it, but it darted out of reach again. He was supposed to leave the window open, as a way out, but he worried because another dragonfly approached from outside. He hurried to the dresser, opened the top drawer, and flung underthings out, as if looking for the money. The next drawer he treated the same way but had to close it a little to pull out the bottom drawer, where he had been told J hid his cash.

B told him J set some kind of trap so he would know if anyone touched his money, an invisible thread or something, but it didn't matter now because he was taking it. He moved a pair of sweat pants and a sweater aside carefully, and saw it—a fat stack, hundreds, maybe thousands, B said. He took the stack in his hand, but when he pulled it out, he heard a snap, like a big rubber band breaking, and something sprayed in his face.

He blinked until he could see again, and wiped at his eyes with his free hand. When he looked in the mirror atop of the dresser, he had thick green paint all over his face. He wanted to wash it off, but J would be in the bathroom, B told him, sitting on the pot and reading the paper as he did every day when he came home from work. He had to get the gun too, a chrome thing with a short barrel. He checked himself in the mirror and noticed the dragonfly hovering behind him, high and to one side. He found this disturbing but had yet to sneak down the hallway and into the living room, on his way to the kitchen.

As he came around the corner into the living room, he saw B in workout clothes, jumping and kicking her legs, her back to him. She wore ear buds, listening to music he could not hear. He snuck in the kitchen, as he had been told. In order to climb in the thin pantry, he had to set the pistol on the counter. Once inside, the door would not close all the way—a bit tighter than he had been told, especially holding a stack of bills. The door moved with his breathing. He took the axe from his belt and held it in front of him, against the side of the pantry. He heard the footsteps, the opening and closing of the refrigerator, the popping of the tab of a beer he had been told J would want. This was K's cue to leap from the pantry and bring the axe down on J's head.

He heard J saying, "What the..." and when he peeked out of the pantry, he saw J taking a swing at the dragonfly. J looked large, his hand almost closing on the dragonfly. It moved out of reach and J took a step closer to the pantry in an effort to catch it. When he did, he saw K's eye in the crack between the door and the pantry and pulled the door wide.

"Who are you?" he asked. K figured it was now or never so he squirmed out of the closet and tried to raise the axe over his head. "And what do you think you're doing?" J demanded, as he snatched the axe out of K's hand. B turned and watched in horror at what she saw: her husband studying the axe in his hand, K looking terrified, his face covered in green paint.

J turned to her. "Did you have something to do with this?"

It was B's turn to feel horror as the dragonfly approached her, hovering just above her head. She took a swipe at it, it dodged out of the way and returned to its original position. "What have you got all over your face?" she screamed. Embarrassed, K wiped at his face with his free hand. He held up the stack of bills to show her he had done something right.

"I got the money," he said.

J looked from B to K. "I would be well within my rights to chop you into little pieces," he said, hefting the axe. K noticed that the dragonfly had approached J from behind, then swung around between them, holding its position above them. J pounded the blunt end of the axe lightly in the palm of his hand. "You gotten that green stuff all over my money."

K tried to imagine a way out of the spot he was in but came up with nothing. He hoped B would think of something, but she stood frozen, arms out at her sides, her mouth and eyes wide and wild. B feared what came next. She knew something of the fury of which J had been capable in the past. He looked at her, and then spun and lunged at K, bringing the axe down firmly on the top of his head. B watched in horror as blood spurted up from his head, as high as the ceiling, as if J had struck a geyser. It took a moment before K collapsed.

J turned, his arms out at his sides in supplication, his face a picture of woe, drenched in K's blood to the chest, with as yet no staunching of the flow in sight. When he tried to get out of the kitchen, J's feet slipped on the blood on the tile floor and he went down like a chopped tree, even his hands slipping as he tried to break his fall. His chin hit sharply, sending sparks and stars and planets swirling around his head. B hurried to his side, kicked him firmly in the head. When she saw the pistol lying on the counter, she grabbed it and set it to J's temple.

"I hope you enjoy this," she said. She pulled the trigger, and though startled by the loud report, she fired again. His head broke in two, like an egg, tiny flames began licking out of the crevice. A dragonfly swept past her head. She threw the pistol back at K, who lay splayed on the floor. She had told K to leave the window open, and now she ran back to the bedroom, tracking bloody footprints behind her. Half a dozen dragonflies hummed and flitted about the bedroom. She swatted them aside, pulled herself onto the sill, and rolled out on her feet, landing with her arms out for balance, ready to fight or flee.

She turned sideways through the hedge into the yard of the building behind theirs. It occurred to her she could scream, get someone to follow her back to the house to find J and K on the kitchen floor, both deceased, presumably at the other's hand. Then she remembered the only way in was through the window. She didn't want to have to climb through it again, with all those dragonflies buzzing around in there. They gave her the creeps.

What she thought she'd do instead is pretend to be jogging. She ran around the building and into the street. It was a warm day, so no one would think twice about a jogger. She waved at a man getting out of his car on the other side of the street. He stopped, watching her run past. Her dancercise must have been paying off. A dog barked behind, a long-haired black and white breed coming after her, so she picked up the pace. The dog matched her, snapping at her ankles.

When she looked down, she noticed her tennis shoes had turned red, and her white socks were also splotched with red. She glanced behind to see several more dogs following. She heard booming from down the street, where she saw young people in uniform coming toward her, each one carrying a terrifying instrument, large black plumes on their hats. The dogs gained on her as Firestone High School band came marching up the street. She dodged into their ranks, crossing through the band to the other side of the street.

Musicians fell in waves as she ran between houses, vaulted over a chain link fence, and came onto the high school grounds, where the team practiced for the big game. She ran up in the bleachers and sat down half-way up to watch them crashing into each other. She heard sirens in the distance as the bleachers began to fill. The team ran off the field, and into the gymnasium, to wait their entrance. She could feel the excitement building toward the game. "Go, Falcons," she whispered.

She wanted to get a hot dog and a drink but was a little shy of showing off her red shoes, so she slipped them off and let them fall through the bleachers. The socks followed, and then she recalled she didn't have any cash on her. As dusk fell, the band came booming back on the field, marching up and down while she clapped with excitement. Then came the cheerleaders tumbling onto the field, and the team broke through a round paper sign with a huge falcon on it. And the kickoff and the passing back and forth, the young bodies smashing against each other. The lights, and when the home team won, a fabulous fireworks display.

# BIRDS OF THUNDER

I GOT THE diagnosis Monday, August 13, 2001—non-Hodgkin's Lymphoma: I would not live out another year. Though this proved not to be the case, it succeeded, understandably, in disturbing me. Mine was not the first false diagnosis in history and will not be the last. I want to note that Harriet Mardock (1958-2001) was a good doctor whose office was conveniently located in my building. Though I credit her with a major change in my lifestyle, after that fateful appointment I went back to work, on the 93rd floor of the World Trade Center, somewhat depressed, not telling a soul of my diagnosis.

Life had an unreality the next couple of weeks, as if I had already died and could not touch anything. So, when the letter from our attorney, Harold Tecopa, arrived Wednesday, September fifth—five days in transit—at my work address, I opened it with little curiosity. It informed me that my grandfather, Archibald Ashton, had been missing for several weeks and is now presumed dead.

I put the letter back in the envelope with every intention of telling Mr. Tecopa I would not run out as soon as possible to settle the estate, and whatever else they wanted me to do, and would not be making the journey in the foreseeable future, but I had a double vision. I had a glimpse of what it meant that I would no longer walk the streets of New York City or any of the many streets of this world; I blinked out of existence, came back remembering what I had double seen and double felt: the world without me and my regret that I would not be there anymore. And I saw my grandfather as I had seen him as a child, a teenager, and a college student: an absent-minded, serious, clean-shaven, dusty man in khaki shirt and pants, work boots and black frame glasses—not a hair on his head.

Papa Archie's skull had an odd forehead bulge not unlike the bulge in my own. Though I understand that male pattern baldness derives from the mother's side, my head is as clean of hair as his then. Once when father left us alone in the house, we bumped into each other in the foyer; he stared and rubbed his head as if looking in a mirror that reflected through time rather than space. I rubbed my head to increase the illusion. He pulled at his nose and warned me not to become so involved in meaningless pursuits that my true work remained undone.

After work, I had a drink with Spring Waits and Will Tom, as we called William Thomas, my very closest friends in the office, to let them know I would be gone for a week to settle grandfather's small estate in the desert. I had mentioned Papa more than once and now I set a photograph of his house in the desert on the table as we sipped scotch.

"When were you last there, Ray?" Spring asked.

"Never," I said. I shrugged at them. "Never in my life."

"Never?"

I shook my head, surprised to dislodge a tear from my left eye.

"Papa Archie visited from time to time," I told them. "Last time, for my Dad's funeral—eight years ago."

"I didn't realize your father had died," said Will Tom, "the way you speak of him."

"We did not always get along."

"You were closer with your mother," Will said.

"No, not at all. My mother died when I was young. In the Congo."

Will wrinkled his brow a bit, and Spring held his drink halfway to his mouth.

"She was engaged in some sort of research there. I don't know what, I am embarrassed to say. We never lived there. She flew back and forth and one day her plane went down over the jungle. Last we knew of her."

"She disappeared?" Spring asked.

It gave me pause, but I nodded. "She disappeared as well."

"My God, man, don't you go disappearing on us," he said, and both of them laughed.

I watched them laugh and then said, "Oh, I won't."

"But your father didn't just disappear, did he?  I hope *he* at least had an honest death."

"Oh, yes.  Cancer.  Smoked a pipe, like my grandfather, all his life.  Papa Archie insisted we lay him out in his dress white uniform.  Said he looked like an angel militant."

"Well, let's have another drink then, to the angel militant!" Will said, and so we did, and bid each other farewell on the sidewalk.

I took Friday off to pack my bags and see my girlfriend Cicely.  We had been seeing each other off and on for a couple of months, but our relationship had not yet progressed far enough to call it serious.  To be sure, it had been slowly moving in that direction.  I had decided not to mention my diagnosis until I returned.

Cicely, six years my junior, worked on my floor and usually wore a suit and round glasses that gave her a charmingly severe appearance, even with her hair loose.  When she opened the door of her condo, I hardly recognized her: dark hair pulled back in a pony-tail, blue shirt open at the top, soft, faded jeans, bare feet, quite lovely, no glasses and such pale brown-gold eyes.

"Come in," she said, as I stood gawking.  I smelled something delicious.  I entered, she shut the door; the rest is a memory I shall never describe in full lest I lose a tiny fraction.  Next morning, I woke in her sunlit bedroom, happier than I have ever been, for anything I can recall. At breakfast, when I suggested I might not fly out west, she insisted I go ahead.

"Family is important, Ray," she said, licking her fingers. "Everything will still be here when you return.  You can count on it."

She drove me to the airport and waved as I boarded the plane.

Because my flight to Kansas City was over three hours and my legs a bit long to sit cramped the whole time, I purchased a first-class ticket.  I felt a bit melancholy when I settled in, so ordered a gin and tonic and read more of the book Will had loaned me when he learned of my appointment with Dr. Mardock, when I first went to her. It was an old hardback from his sci-fi collection: *No Other Man,* by Alfred Noyes. It pleased me that the scientist in the novel was a Dr. Mardok.

The fellow in the next seat got his ticket as a gift from his parents in K.C. because he had just finished his PhD in Post-Modern Technology. At six-three, he needed that extra space. An appealing young man in a pony-tail and beard, he had a freshness I enjoyed. I bought him a drink, another for myself, and listened to his discourse on The Loud Speaker, its place and meaning in our lives, beginning with the megaphone.

"Do you read science fiction, Travis?" I asked him when he seemed to have finished.

He shook his head. "Not really."

"This fellow, this Dr. Mardok, invents a death ray that wipes out the human race. How's that for post-modern technology?"

"Chilling," he said and sipped the last of his drink.

The alcohol contributed to a desolate mood as I thought of Cicely, far behind me now in New York City. I drifted into uneasy sleep and woke a couple of hours later to climb aboard a big-bellied converted mail transport plane with a large propeller on each wing, wondering if this too was part of a dream.

I watched from the window as stranger parts of this country passed beneath me, our own shadow crossing the fields and waters below. I boarded yet another, smaller plane, nine seats on a side, no moving air. My companions, a family of dark, silent Indians, and a fellow who tipped his cowboy hat over his eyes and went to sleep, did not comfort me on a bumpy ride.

I no longer knew where I was when I stepped onto the short metal stairway pulled to the door. I waited for other passengers to deplane so I could straighten my clothes, tie my shoes, and lock my carry-on bag. By the time I stepped down onto the narrow runway, I was the only person in sight—unless you count the dark range rover speeding off over the desert in the distance.

It was hot as a brick oven. As I walked toward a small building in the distance, a big dark man on a horse, a rawhide thong around his head, came trotting toward me. He trailed another without a rider. My eyes watered a bit in fear until he stopped and called, "Archie?"

I shaded my eyes, looking up at him.

He swung his leg over his horse and dropped to the ground with a thud. When he stuck his huge hand out to me, he said, "Howard Tecopa, your grandpa's attorney."

He looked uncertain until I nodded and put out my own hand to be swallowed in his.

"Ray Ashton. Pleased to meet you."

He took a bandana from his back pocket and wiped his forehead.

"Hot like hell out here, ain't it?"

"As a matter of fact."

He took a couple of plastic bottles of water from his saddle bag and handed me one.

"Was the trip too bad?"

"Long."

We both drank greedily and wiped our mouths while we studied each other.

"You look just like your grandpa," he said. "A little younger." Then he looked up at the sun, halfway down in the west. "Well, we don't want to get caught out in the dark, so we better get along. You climb on Little Bit there."

With that, he swung back up onto the horse and reached down for my bag. I handed it to him and watched as he attached it to his saddle horn.

"I'm not much of a horseman," I told him.

"Little Bit there will do all the work."

After a few failed attempts, I got my leg up over the horse and my butt in the saddle and we trotted along. Once past the shed we broke into a gallop, and I just hoped I could stay on the horse's back.

"Just relax and you'll do fine," he said. Tecopa had his head turned back to watch me, and when he thought I might make it, he turned around again.

He said nothing the whole way.

68

I did try to relax, but I felt constant tension through my body until I saw the yellow house approaching in the distance.

When he pulled up beside it, my horse slowed to a stop. I was so stiff and shakey, I fell to my knees when I touched ground. I stayed a moment looking at the house, as if it was a mirage. By the time I stood, Tecopa had gone in the front door with my bag.

Inside, the house was one main room, a living room with a huge desk against a wall and a kitchen area where Tecopa stood, wiping his dripping face on a towel.

"I caught a couple trout this morning. I'll fry them up if you're hungry."

"Starved."

"I stocked the fridge with beers if you'd like one."

In a short time, I sat at Papa Archie's table having trout, flatbread, corn-on-the-cob, and a beer with Tecopa. Everything else, the whole mess of my life, was gone, nowhere to be found. I was nothing but me in this house in the desert. We ate with our heads down. When we finished and had another beer, I felt restored.

"That was good," I said.

Tecopa smiled and nodded. "Many's the time I sat here with your grandpa like this." He held up the beer and nodded. "A fine fella, your grandpa." He took another long swig, downing the rest of the beer. "You'll want to step outside now that it's dark."

He got up from the table and nodded toward the door. "Come on," he said. "You're going to like this."

As I followed, I realized it had gotten dark in a short time, and the second thing I noticed was the enormous blue-black sky, splashed and swirling with stars. As I watched I saw a falling star, and in another moment a second. I could feel the quiet all around me.

"Nothing like this in New York," he said.

"No," I said. "Is it always like this?"

"You bet."

We watched the sky several minutes before I heard a distant yipping sound.

"Coyotes," said Tecopa. "Hunting for anything they can get."

"Anything?"

"Oh, they'll most likely leave you alone," he said, and then he laughed. "Well, I better be getting home to Marg. She'll be wondering what happened to me." He shook my hand, gave me a bright smile, and got on his horse. Before he rode off, he asked if I went to church, and when I told him not really, he whistled and turned the horse.

I could actually see him for quite a while, before he disappeared into a dark inky spot. I heard yipping, more distant now, and above me the dome of night. Little Bit shifted and startled me. I didn't know what I should do for the horse, so I went in and turned on as many lights as I could, but that made me feel vulnerable. From outside, anyone could have seen the house for miles.

I called Cicely to tell her about my trip and hear her laughter, but nothing happened, no tone, nothing.

Only thing left to do, turn off the lights and go to sleep. I pulled the blanket and sheet off the bed to check for spiders and scorpions, and then took the bedding to the main room and wrapped myself like a mummy on the couch.

It was then that I remembered I was scheduled to die.

When I woke on Sunday, September 9, to daylight, I pulled back the blue curtain to see Little Bit still standing beside the house. I felt guilty for doing nothing for him. I ground beans and made a pot of coffee, and went outside to pee on the ground.

Outside, I stretched and sat a while in the outdoor John. The air had a touch of coolness. If I had known a thing about riding I might have taken Little Bit out. At just the thought of riding out in the desert, I experienced a terror.

I poured a mug of coffee and wandered around the main room of the house.

At the other end from the kitchen was a huge fireplace made of large rocks, obviously used regularly. No mantel, nothing on the wall to the stucco ceiling. A couple of rifles stood in the corner, and a row of windows ran the length of the wall against which the couch stood, with short blue curtains on hoops.

On the other side of the room, Papa Archie's desk, files, cupboard. A rather ugly painting above the desk pictured some prehistoric winged creature, maybe a pterodactyl. Then I noticed a few more drawings of the same bird stuck to the cupboard.

As I compared them, I became certain that whoever did the painting had not also done the cruder, if more scientific drawings. When I opened the files, I came first on one tagged *Archie III* and found perhaps fifty letters from my own father, so I poured another mug and sat at the table reading these epistles from Dad.

We had not had much of a relationship in his last five, maybe even ten years. I suppose then I thought he would live forever and there would be time to get to know him once I'd made him feel my anger for a sufficient length of time. I'd been making my own career as well. I'd like to blame more on him than I do, but reading these letters did not help.

Dad spoke glowingly of my accomplishments, and of his hopes for me. Tears obscured the words and I had to lower my head and weep. I kept seeing Daddy in that dress white uniform in the coffin, Papa weeping, calling him Angel Militant.

I sat until I read every one from beginning to end, surprised that Dad kept up with Papa's scientific discussions, interested in whatever discoveries Papa claimed to be making. I noted mentions of the Thunder Bird, but could not tell from the context whether Dad meant a car, an aircraft, or an actual beast. I saw crude sketches of the bird-like creature tacked on Papa's cupboards in my father's hand, with suggestions about how the jointures in the wings might work—as I understood it.

I had been reduced to a child overhearing this conversation between Dad and Grand-Dad. I tried calling Cicely, failed.

When I heard horses' hooves, I jumped up and ran to the front door, my heart pounding. Tecopa was already coming off his horse, behind him a woman and two children on horseback.

"Howdy," he called. "I brought my wife and kids to meet you."

"You are all welcome."

Once they dismounted, he introduced me to his wife Marg, Richard his oldest, and Betty his daughter. I was relieved that Richard tended to Little Bit, as the rest of us went in. As Marg and Howard fixed dinner, he said, "The way you ate that trout last night I thought you might like a little more of the same, made Marg's special way."

A short woman with the darkest eyes I have ever seen, Marg wore a white peasant blouse with little red flowers dotting the top, and like all of them blue jeans and boots. They came from church and she said it was all they could do to make their friends stay home today. "The kids loved your grandpa. They were excited to meet you."

With a forkful of fish halted before his mouth, Tecopa told me the council met right after church to launch a full-scale search for Papa Archie.

"If they can't find him, no one will." In went the fish, but he kept smiling, pointing his fork at me. "I told you, all it would take was for you to come out here."

"They need a nudge," Marg said. "Or they just do what they always do, go on with their lives. That's how people are."

Richard wanted to show me Archie's Lizard, as he called it, so later that afternoon, with plenty of water in our saddle bags, we rode out in bright sunlight. Everything looked the same out there to me, but they knew where they were going, up the bare hill a decent distance behind the house, through scrub, yellow flowers, little creatures like dry chipmunks scurrying about, strange birds I had never seen, lizards I saw as an indication of what lay ahead.

"Keep an eye out for rattlers," Howard warned. We dismounted and left the horses to crawl through a narrow pass and under a cave-like tunnel to a wide, flat section literally cut out of the hill, a rocky abutment. I saw nothing until Richard said, "See his back?" I saw only ruts and cut-outs in the hill, and then I saw the backbone Richard pointed out.

"That's Grandpa Archie's Lizard," said Betty. She smiled and hid herself behind Marg, except for her eyes.

"See the head," Howard said, outlining it from a distance with his finger.

It emerged slowly for me, until the creature lay before me as it had in life and in death.

"Is it a dragon?" I said, and when they laughed, I felt foolish and laughed at myself.

Marg clapped her hands in glee. "It was hard to believe you didn't see it right away, but if you don't expect it, you might not see it. It jumps right out at us."

"It chases us in our dreams," said Richard.

"I call him Squiggly," said Betty.

"Archie spent months coming to clear this fellow," said Howard. "I came sometimes with food and water. He'd forget everything to work. Once I found him passed out, and I think he might have died if I hadn't given him water and carried him back to the house."

Howard shook his head. "That's the way it is for a great man," he said.

"You think he was a great man?" I asked.

They all looked at me. "You didn't know?" Richard asked.

"I've been working in New York all this time."

Howard told his kids, "Ray here works in the tallest building in the world."

Already, it seemed so long ago, and so meaningless.

We stood in silence a while before Archie's Lizard. On the way back, we saw a few more fossils and when we got home, more food and drink, a fire outside, and stories of those Birds of Thunder. Howard's hands swooped gracefully when the birds made an appearance.

Next morning, I shooed spiders and watched a lizard cross the ceiling and come down the wall as I sat at Papa's desk going through his papers. I had a little better idea of what he was doing here, alone in the desert. Time passed without awareness until the ache for

Cicely throbbed, recalling our last night, waking in the morning beside her.

I couldn't even get her a message by email, with no service. Time was short, I told myself. I would leave as soon as my business here was done. I became impatient.

Little Bit was outside, but I didn't feel confident about riding into the desert. Minutes and hours passed until at three in the afternoon I heard galloping hooves and went out to see if Howard had returned. The group approached at top speed. Tecopa broke from seven dark men, leaping off his horse while the rest waited, circling, pacing. All of them had rifles slung on their saddles.

"We found him." He pointed off in the distance.

"Alive?"

"Of course not," he said. "Let's go."

Reluctantly, I climbed on Little Bit. I did not want to upset this difficult day by finding my deceased grandfather.

As we moved down a steep declivity, I leaned back in my saddle to offset the angle of the descent. I had no idea such a descent existed out here, or where we would end up. None of the men spoke, though water bottles passed among us and dust rose into our eyes and mouths. I tied a bandana Howard tossed me across my mouth and depended on tears in my eyes to clear them. All the water in my body had been squeezed out by the heat when we made level ground, perhaps an hour into the journey.

I noticed more brush down here, fewer creatures scurrying about. A lone coyote watched us pass, and finally we came to an area of huge rocks and rising ground.

"It's in here," Howard said. We dismounted and I followed him through boulders while the others waited for us.

"You go on," Howard said. "Go on ahead. He's there."

I picked my way through brambles and scrub, into a cave-like face of rock and earth that had been chipped away, revealing the head of an enormous creature emerging from one side of a rise as if it came at me. I saw the tools scattered about, lying on the ground, and something like a large green-brown pack on the ground right in front of me.

I went to one knee and touched it. My body shook as I realized I had touched a leg. The body had curled into itself, knees raised partway to the chest, arms tucked in, all dried and baked by the sun, only the faintest of dry odors rising off the body. I leaned over him to look into his face, but it wasn't until I saw the bulge in his forehead I knew it was Papa. I was so far beyond tears I simply sat down beside him and waited for I don't know what. When I remembered the men waiting for me, I crawled out of the brush and through the crevice, unable to stand as they all watched me coming. When I stood and looked up at Howard, I asked him what we should do with the body. He shrugged.

"Why not leave him here, now that we know where he is. It's a good spot."

When Howard looked up, I followed his gaze to the cliff behind us. I stared at it for a while, and then I nodded. "Sure," I said. "That sounds right."

Next morning, I hopped on Little Bit and went out by myself. I left a note, in case I got lost. I had strapped on my watch for security and hung Papa's powerful binoculars around my neck. I did not go down the incline this time but rode to the top of the cliff I had seen from below.

I had a terrible fear of heights at that time, a disadvantage considering where I worked. My soul plunged and rose through my body, out the top of my head as I approached the edge. Astride Little Bit, overlooking a vast desert of which Papa Archie was now a part, my own mortality perched awkwardly on my shoulders, threatening to pitch me forward into eternal doom or exhilaration.

I sat there until the visceral reaction to the height died down, and I was at peace. When I dared glance down at my watch, it was eight forty-five. In the distance I saw two birds with an enormous wing span. If vultures, they were closer than they appeared. I lifted the binoculars to my eyes. I knew at that moment: my life would never be the same. But as usual, we mistake or fail to understand all of the information we are receiving at any moment until much later.

Here, I thought the Death Ray had been aimed at me. I did not know it was not my future which had ended but my past. I know that mine was not the first false diagnosis in the world, nor will it be the last. But, my dear Dr. Mardock, what strange design has brought me here I cannot name. At times I almost believe that this is nothing more than an incomprehensible afterlife.

# AMONG THE MEEP

I DID NOT know Margaret before we arrived against our wills, totally in the dark. We tumbled out, then sat up and evaluated each other a moment before we heard movement in the undergrowth, followed by the face of a strange man peering through the green and purple foliage—black hair, streaked with white, and those pale blue eyes jumping from one to the other of us. He must have thought quite a while what to say, appealing to our desire for restoration of a sense of normalcy.

"The plane is this way," he said. "If you'll follow me, we can try to get out of this God forsaken place."

Nothing truly made sense, but, nevertheless, we both stood, Margaret carrying a pair of high heel shoes, and squeezed through the underbrush behind this slender fellow in loose safari clothing, a sidearm and hunting knife strapped to either hip. He lacked only the pith helmet to complete the image of the British colonizer. He rattled what I know now as nonsense along the way: "My pilot died tragically in the crash landing, right through the windshield. I do have some rudimentary knowledge of flying, map and compass. I'm sure I can get the little craft on course with the help of even a novice navigator."

The sun had come up, light spreading through trees and undergrowth. Any remaining chill of darkness fled; the jungle about us commenced steaming. We were quite hot, sweating when we passed through a wide clearing where the sun beat down with a particular fury. The air wavered with the heat. Our guide mopped his neck with a soiled handkerchief and displaced the silence by telling us, "I worked all day yesterday as well as the day before putting this thing back together. And the day before that I'm afraid."

Margaret inquired how far we had yet to go in this heat. "Not much further," he said. He stopped and turned to us. "I hate to say this but there won't be room for three of us on the plane. One of you will stay behind. Once we find our way out, I'll come back for the other."

Margaret and I looked at each other. It was obvious I should remain behind, but Margaret volunteered right away. The stranger gave me a steely stare, from which I concluded that he too assumed I should remain behind rather than Margaret.

"No, no," I said. "Of course, I will remain behind."

"I will leave a rifle with you," he quickly asserted, "for self-defense."

"What nonsense," Margaret said. "I am quite adept at wilderness survival and will remain behind. I am something of a marksman, no doubt a better shot than this fellow."

"This arrangement is unacceptable," said the stranger. "I must insist you remain behind."

Here he looked pointedly at me.

"I am in complete agreement," I said, underscoring the point by removing my tie.

"But I am not." Margaret dropped her heels to the ground and let it be known that on this point she would stand her ground. The stranger drew his pistol, for all the world like an old six shooter. "It should be clear that survival is the issue in our present environment. I will take the lady to civilization and return for you."

"I won't go," Margaret insisted. "You'll have to shoot me with that ridiculous pistol if you continue to insist."

She took a few steps toward him, and I watched with fascination as she set her hand on top of the one holding the pistol. "I think we both know, if there is indeed a plane ahead, either you have not been working on it or it will not fly, as you have neither grease nor oil on your soft hands."

"I am warning you."

"Since I will do no good for you dead, I assume you meant to shoot him," and here she pointed at me, "maim him or tie him up, and take me off for what you are craving."

He glanced down at the hand she inserted in his shirt. She extended her tongue in a most insinuating manner, and then, in an instant, he lay on the ground, her bare foot on his throat, the tip of the barrel of his own pistol pressed to his forehead. When the explosion came, the bloody stub of his head opened as if it had burst from inside.

We found his camp near a river, the tent roomy enough to contain camp table and chairs, a wide cot, a lamp run off batteries, and an assortment of books and papers. Also, a large metal box that from time to time emitted chirping sounds in apparent attempt to communicate with our former guide. His camp was well stocked, as if he had just arrived or received a delivery. Three pairs of women's shoes lined up against a large trunk gave me pause.

Like Goldilocks, Peggy tried all three, one too large, one too small, the third just right, each pair sturdy enough for the serious work of survival. In the trunk she discovered a trove of clothing from which she furnished a wardrobe of safari style to match those I had taken from our guide. Outfitted with one of the rifles, she led us out to explore our new home. Though we found no evidence of a plane, we did discover what amounted to a boneyard—a clearing scattered with bones, hair, and such.

A man has to eat, no surprises there, but these bones—of brown and yellow and white, baking and baked in the sun—presented an all too recognizable aspect, indicated by the presence of human or human-like skulls broken at crown and temple. The absence of an offensive smell spoke to the heat of the noonday sun and the marvelous influence of the air. "It appears," I told her, "that you have done us a real service blowing that fellow's head off."

My eyes are as blue as our guide's, hers golden brown and almond in shape. We looked at each other several minutes, recognizing racial differences in our appearance. How we came to this particular pass, neither knew, but we stood together over the shambles, a gathering of bloody bones, understanding how much we now depended on each other.

Our discussion turned to the discovery of other creatures, arriving at a decision to check the narrow river for fish or other aquatic life. Thus, we went back to camp to study the pellucid water of a river with only minor rills on the surface though it rushed at quite a pace. At first the only life we could ascertain came in the form of extremely large tadpoles. We took off footwear and dangled our toes in the river. Because it was so hellishly hot, the cool water came as a balm to the soul, and I said so, which made Peggy laugh.

But then, the expression on her face made me look around. The wings were translucent, with purple veins running through, blending with the background green. I had read of prehistoric varieties with a wingspan as much as four or five feet, but this dragonfly measured greater than six, hovering a moment before flitting to the opposite bank of the river with a great thrumming which fell silent as it hovered again. It dipped down and touched water, rose and dipped again.

I had not noticed that Peggy had shed her clothes until she waded in the river. She ducked under and came up smoothing back her dark, now sparkling hair. I watched her a moment before I too shed my clothes. I left the knife on the bank in case I should need it quickly.

The crowd of tadpoles that gathered around made us laugh at their wriggling antics. It was at this point I saw an enormous frog across the river, sitting impassively. I mentioned the tadpoles were large, but to approximate the size of this green and purple spotted creature, I would have to compare it in height to a large horse, in girth to the hippopotamus.

Needless to say, we hurried from the water for fear this thing might jump in with us. We lay on shore, hearts pumping fast and hard. Two more huge frogs appeared at the side of the first and set up a horrible croaking. It took a while to become convinced they took no notice of us, but they provided a moment of horror when one shot out its long, purple tongue to wrap around one of the dragonflies. The wings crackled and buckled on their way into its mouth.

We forced ourselves to eat some dried meat that proved less chewy than I feared, perhaps due to the heat of the afternoon. We sat under the tarp at the tent entrance, sipping tea. Every-once-in-a-while we heard the chirping box in the tent. Only a few hours of sunlight remained, so we set out in the direction we had come this morning, skirting the clearing where our former guide baked in his underwear, his blunt and bloodied head rammed in the soil.

We traced the way we had first come until we found the thicket where our journey began, alarmed that dusk arrived sooner than expected. I looked up to see the large shadow that had her attention: a wide, gray circular shape that stood on tripod legs coming down through the trees. I located the metal container, like the claw of some earthbound crane, from which we had dropped to the jungle floor, at the end of a retractable arm.

At this point, Peggy and I hurried back to the tent, shivering in the cold of the evening, looking about for what hid in the night. We zipped ourselves in the tent, wakeful and agitated. Throughout the night we remained vigilant. If Peggy slept in the wide cot in which our former guide once slept, I stayed awake, pistol at the ready. Occasionally the metal box chirped, and I heard sounds in the night but could not make out any of them and could not be sure they were not the products of enlivened imagination.

When we woke next morning, I felt clear-headed, pleased with myself until the chirping started up with greater frequency as we took our cup of tea. We tried to ignore the communicator until it worried at us that whoever chirped at our former guide might decide to pay an unwanted visit.

The thing possessed surprising weight. We carried it precariously between us, stepping sideways through the brush until we reached river's edge. Once we had found the deepest spot, it sank swiftly to the pebbly bottom, chirping another five minutes, sending up a stream of bubbles until it ceased. Having disposed of the communicator, we feared some chirping might be going on in the craft that dropped us off the previous morning. We easily found our way through the beaten-down flora, though I could see it had begun restoring its former growth. We passed our former guide in the position we left him, his skin darkened and drawn back from eyeballs and teeth. Thankfully, he did not have the fetid smell of the dead.

When we reached the immense tripod legs, an energetic wide-leafed vine encircled them, creating an effective ladder for our journey upward, hampered only by the long axe Peggy carried and the blunt force instrument under my belt. I felt like Jack of the beanstalk as we climbed stout vines, holding on overhead with occasional dips and snapping offshoots that gave a scare. These vines ended close enough to reach the hatch from which a crane arm descended to the metal box in which we had been lowered.

I calmed my shaking arms, and, climbing as quickly as I could, clambered into the hatch, to lay a moment before crawling forward to allow the entrance of Peggy. Our breathing echoed in the dark. I could see nothing, not even my hand before me. I feared we would have a hard time feeling our way until a beam of light pierced through above me. It gave me a start until I realized Peggy brought the flashlight.

At last, we both stood and searched the cavity until we found the metal ladder into a second hatch above, which I opened with my shoulders. In the heart of the craft I could barely stand, but light poured in from windows above so we could clearly see the circular interior and an array of levers, gears, and switches. I took the mallet from my belt, wondering where to begin, when we heard chirping from a central area of the panel. Peggy attacked it with her axe until the guts of the thing sprung back, striking her forehead. She fell back, and in that terrible moment I saw blood on her forehead. "Peggy," I called, "are you all right?"

She glared at me before she leapt back at the panel and began slashing. I joined at another vulnerable port and soon had the wreckage at my feet, the only sound our own heavy breathing. We looked at each other and began to laugh. I slid the mallet in my belt and she sheathed the ax head in the holster on hers. "Now," she said, "how do we get down?"

Fortunately, we found the elevator that went down through the widest of the three legs to the jungle floor. Though we had just rendered it thoroughly inoperable, we managed to repel by holding the braided cable, literally walking down the leg.

Sweaty, filthy, nearly inexplicable blood on our hands and face, all we could think of was getting back to the river. When we once more passed the even drier corpse of our guide, I vowed to return to bury him. But, having conceived of relief in the river, we raced the rest of the way.

Discarding clothes as quickly as possible, we plunged in and swam about with eyes open. Clarity underwater was, if anything, greater than on the land. The tadpoles were noticeably more mature than the day before. We caught sight of a long, thick fish-type creature passing along the other side of the river. It had three nodules, bumps you might call them, on its side, where a wide purple stripe went from the head to the split or forked tail which whipped about in what looked like a circular motion. It seemed to watch us with doleful, bulbous eyes. We attempted to follow, but it wriggled its body once and shot far out of sight.

As we treaded water, Peggy noticed the communicator did not seem to be where we left it. We dressed and hurried back to the safety of camp. To our shock, the communicator sat beside our camp chairs, dripping water.

As afternoon progressed, I decided it was time I go back and do my duty to the dead man, a task for which Peggy had no stomach. I set out with pick, shovel, canvas tarp, and a thermos of water. When I stood beside him, the smell of his body was as the scent of museums. He was less a man now than a desiccated artifact of this monstrous world.

I spread the tarp beside the body and attempted to swing the shoulders onto it when the head rolled against my legs, rocking a moment before it stilled. The shoulders lay at an angle on the tarp, so I took the legs at the calf and swung them onto the tarp. Unfortunately, the body broke at the waist. Once I got all the parts gathered in the middle, I drew the corners of the tarp together and carried it on my back. Slick with sweat, I arrived at the shambles to unfurl my load onto the pile he no doubt had a hand in accumulating.

I leaned against a green and purple thing I called a tree, possessed of the living scent of decay. I began to notice many but not all of the bones had a human aspect; others were thinner, frailer. My first thought was these were the bones of children, but they had a lacy appearance. I handled a few of the lighter bones, breaking them easily.

That's when I saw the green lizard, its long, yellow tongue flickering, testing and tasting the air. It rose from a pile of bones and descended again, only to rise further on. When it came to the head of our guide, bumping its active tongue through an eyehole, it found what remained of the moist brains.

That evening, I didn't feel like talking, and neither did she, so we sat by a low fire until it grew dark, our weapons on our knees, the night bright with stars. A high moon was at half—only the bottom half visible—and a lower moon at full. "I saw a bird," she said, "when I went to answer the call of nature. Squatting on the hole I dug, I saw a tall bird hopping through the trees."

"What color?"

"Brown, I think, and purple."

"It would be worth knowing more of this bird."

She looked serious then and stood up, her rifle at the ready.

"What is it?" I whispered, standing beside her.

Though the moons gave some dim light, we could barely see trees and bushes in the odd shadows. It was as if the shadows had taken shape low in the trees, moving toward us, stepping into the moonlight. Twenty or twenty-five creatures half our size stood before us, their arms at their sides somewhat darker than their bodies. The moonlight made their skin look wet. They kept coming toward us until they stopped in a body no more than ten yards away. One of them spoke clearly, saying, "Meep." A few others took up the sound, then silence.

Peggy returned the sound. "Meep," she said, confirming the shape of the sound. It now occurred to me they might be telling us the name of their planet. I kneeled, placed one hand on the ground, and said, "Meep?"

At first, the creatures stiffened, but they seemed to take great interest in my gesture. The one in front kneeled also, though I could not be certain they had knees at the moment. One of his dark arms went out and touched the ground as well. "Cang," he said.

"Cang," I repeated.

All of them repeated the sound and got down in a position I call kneeling. Peggy kneeled beside me and said, "Cang." Then she leaned forward in a posture that alarmed me, touching her forehead to the ground. To lend support, I followed her example.

When we looked up again, the host before us returned the gesture.

The front fellow raised his mouth hole high and gave a long ululation that echoed back through the throng as they all followed suit. When at last they fell silent, in order to respond, I sang to them: "Row, row, row your boat." Peggy came in on the third *row*, completing the round: "Gently down the stream, merrily, merrily, merrily, merrily, life is but a dream."

Peggy finished after I did and the creatures set up a horrifying din. "Is that applause," she wondered aloud, "or laughter?"

The creatures fell silent as we started again. Once more, when we finished, the throng set up the hideous din. We went through the process eight or nine times at what we presumed was their request. The lead fellow moved toward us, causing me no small apprehension, stopping so close I got a whiff of his scent: parsley.

The series of noises he then emitted had the sound of an explanation, as he touched the silent communicator several times. It occurred to me he was telling us they had found this thing in the river and delivered it to our camp. This much closer, I had opportunity to scrutinize him in detail, realizing this was none other than the fish-creature we had seen swimming past us.

When Peggy said, "I'm sorry if we left it in a place you didn't want left," the fellow fell silent, taking his opportunity to study us.

After a moment of silence, to our astonishment, he sang the tune of "Row, row, row your boat" back to us with weird, discordant sounds replacing words. When we applauded, he backed away a bit, so we stopped just in time to hear the entire gang join in on their version of the song. Still warbling, the beings turned as one, the leader now at the rear, and made their way back to jungle, leaving us with the abiding scent of parsley.

Next day, I took notebook and pencils, heading into deep forest to expand the knowledge of our surroundings and find Peggy's bird. As I wandered, I considered how far from home I had come. I remembered with fondness the little house in which I grew up, my dear mother, my wonderful, fuddled father forever tinkering in his backyard laboratory. As I recalled them, I saw them before me, mother in her cat eye glasses, reddish hair standing straight up in great loops and curls, her red-painted mouth—and then, in a flash, I saw my mother before me.

It took a moment for me to comprehend I had come face to face with the bird of which Peggy spoke, its head tilted downwards, looking down its long beak at me with great eyes. The transformation of the image of my mother into the bird sent a shock through my system, and a jolt of adrenalin made me reach out and grab it by the neck. In no time, I had a wild screeching monster in my hands, the trapped bird beating me with its considerable wings.

"For the love of God," I shouted, "calm down."

The bird fled through underbrush, screeching as it went, and I ran haphazardly through jungle, gasping for air. I could barely see sunlight through the canopy overhead. For a moment, I feared I might never find my way back until I heard the running water of the river. I came to its edge and followed in the bright sun for an hour or so, until I came upon a gorge, around which I saw the Meep lounging and reclining and carrying on their conversations with each other.

Though I had never been so relieved to see anyone, this did not appear to be mutual, as all the Meep leaped into the river. At least a dozen of them swam about among underwater caves and rocky structures like otters. I sat on the bank, my legs crossed, taking some pleasure in their company, even if they remained in the water.

My spirits had lifted when I thought of the pleasure I would have showing this to Peggy. One of the Meep came out of the water, waddled close, and bowed his head to the ground. I too bowed and touched my forehead to the ground.

A friend joined him, and they seemed a bit like friendly penguins as they mimicked the tune of "Row, row, row your boat" in that mildly horrifying voice of theirs. I applauded softly, not to startle them, and sang it back. Soon a group of six or seven joined them, before they lost interest and leaped back in the water.

Nothing now seemed amiss as I followed the river until I arrived at a smaller gorge where a larger creature swam, my own dear Peggy. She had her back to me, treading water as I said her name. She rotated until she saw me. "Did you find my bird?" she called.

"Indeed, I did!"

She swam closer, looking up at me with pure joy that I had returned.

"I also found the place where the Meep make their home," I told her.

That last bit of news excited her. She had taken a fancy to the Meep. I took off my shoes and jumped in with clothes on, which Peggy found terribly funny. "They needed a good wash as well," I said. Then, I climbed out, laid my clothes to dry, and when I turned to leap in, saw them coming through the water. They must have followed me.

I stood naked on the shore—so trusting had I become of our environment—and watched the joy on Peggy's face turn to horror. She screamed as the Meep tore at her from all sides, biting chunks of flesh from bone with a frantic action and a sound that haunts me. Her expression went from horror to dismay, to blankness, to nothing. In minutes, they reduced her to skeleton. Bits of flesh and drifting blood were scooped or sucked down the gullets of the wretched creatures.

I had been frozen in place, only to witness a second horror. Several Meep crawled out of the gorge as those in the water nudged her bones to the bank. These others collected and carried them to the shambles, where marrow would be sucked from bone by lizards. I cannot adequately express the depression into which I fell. She had made the prospect of a lifetime on an unknown planet less full of dread than hope. It took another week to make up my mind to perish as Peggy had, with one leap into the waters of Cang, at the gorge where I found them, leaving behind this testament of our sojourn. You who read this know as much as I can tell from experience.

If you should look for me, seek me in the shambles, among the Meep.

# HEARING IS BELIEVING

BERNARD BARTRAM HAD achieved some notoriety among the unbelieving community, and, therefore, had become notorious in the community of belief. He thought of himself as an expert in the field of unbelief, which tickled him. His defining book, *Unbelieving*, written twelve years earlier in a fit of rational passion—there's an oxymoron for you, he thought—had established his *bona fides*. He followed this two years later, while he was still hot, his publisher told him, with the more painstaking and laborious (to write) *You Can't Be Serious*. These made him a welcome speaker at various clubs and societies for the preservation of unbelief or belief, such as the one he had spoken at this evening, opposite Dr. Ollie Apple, a famous believer.

He sat in an odious dressing room provided by I.I.F. (Institute for the Investigation of Faith) sipping a second glass of Glenlivet on crushed ice, also provided by I.I.F., reflecting on a joke he made during the debate at the expense of his opponent's surname, explaining he hoped to make the good doctor take a bite of his own apple. Though it garnered the expected laughter, it brought him no joy. He had not delved deep to find the line, and it seemed overworked, lacking in the seeming or actual spontaneity of true humor. The dressing room did not help his mood. He sat facing a wall with a three-paneled mirror and a shelf at about waist level, presumably for the application of make-up, though nothing but the scotch and a bowl of ice sat on it. The wall on his right was the original *tabula rasa*, a dirty beige with scars, marks, and scratches in places both inexplicable and uninteresting. To his left, a long closet occupied the wall, lined at intervals with coats and costumes defeating explanation, all dark and unused, as if for centuries.

The wall behind him, the fourth wall, contained nothing but a single door, closed, through which one entered this dismal room, and he saw it only through the bad graces of the speckled mirror. Like the room, this career of his seemed empty now, as it should, he reasoned, given that the position he long ago adopted was unbelief. He felt certain there must be deep irony in being a famous atheist, but no more than in being a celebrated believer whose arguments he could barely recall seconds after Apple spoke them: pure nonsense. For moments that grew longer through the evening, he lost contact with the words spoken by his opponent, irritation growing into various scenarios in which he strangled Apple right there on the stage. His own best moment came when he broke into one of Apple's explanations with the unexpected quip that Dr. Apple was the only human being left in the world who hoped to talk God back into existence. It drove him to despair when Apple leaped into what he obviously considered a clever reversal as he attempted to prove the existence of God through scientific formulations.

Bartram's patience wore thin enough to instruct the audience that Dr. Apple had revealed himself as someone who knew nothing of true science, particularly the second law of thermodynamics, which he had mentioned three times in rapid succession, as if it were a magical incantation. Then, as he fell silent and sullen, Apple droned on, imagining his audience spellbound. To be sure, he did seem to recall several bright episodes of communal laughter during the good doctor's speech, but Bartram himself grew sick and sicker of Apple, of himself, of this charade, nothing more than a ritual repeated before an audience that long ago lost its ability to believe in God, religion having devolved into a set of gang signs, at worst; at best, into empty cliché.

As he poured himself a second scotch on ice and sat back down before the mirror, he had begun to enumerate in his mind each time he had participated in this blank ritual, and for which he had begun to slightly despise himself. Neither he nor Dr. Apple could refrain from this mind-numbing work since they both valued their living quarters and their dinner tables—for Bartram, restaurants— sufficiently to keep them at it. Worse, they both knew this, and during one of those passages in which Ollie had developed another execrable conceit, Bartram recognized the deep boredom this God-bearer to the New World hid beneath a thin veneer of otiose wit, boilerplate scripture, and timeworn phrases in which he had stopped believing years before, if he ever had. The word *effete* applied to both of them: affected, over-refined, and ineffectual.

No one would be saved or damned. They could only hope to entertain, and that had worn so thin at final applause, peppered with cheers, boos, and laughter, that he nearly ran offstage to his ridiculous dressing room to down his first, now third scotch. When he heard a door closing behind him, he looked up, into the mirror, rather than behind, to find a swarthy, diminutive man with fly-away white hair and a thin goatee in a gray-on-gray striped suit. At the throat of a shirt somewhere between white and yellow, he wore a large black bowtie with white polka dots. The man appeared to be a tad embarrassed, holding a worn leather satchel at his knees that strained at the seams with a bulging something secreted inside. Having received his share of death threats and well-wishing encouragements in equal proportion, he had for years awaited the unknown assailant who would step from the shadows and make good on his threat.

"Dr. Bartram," the man whispered, "my name is..." and he said something completely unintelligible to Bartram. Then, he smiled and said, "But you may call me Jesus. I represent the Institute and wish to congratulate you on a sparkling defense of unbelief." He paused and smiled again, his face returning quickly to its slightly apprehensive expression. "I hope you will give me leave a few minutes for a valuable experiment. Valuable to the Institute, potentially to yourself."

"Your name is Jesus?"

"A common name in all cultures but your own."

This so irritated Bartram that he could not speak for several moments, during which time Jesus kept his eyes trained on him, waiting for approval to continue. Bartram rubbed his forehead with two fingers to demonstrate irritation. "Number one, I am not a doctor; number two, I have no notion of which institute you speak. I

91

am now going to refresh my drink, and by the time I am seated once again, I hope you will have the decency of God and make yourself scarce." He began to stand, but the girlish tittering of the man who called himself Jesus surprised Bartram so that he could not move for a moment.

"Oh, Mr. Bartram, you made us laugh tonight. Thank you for your wisdom and humor."

Bartram dropped back in his seat, watching the stranger in the speckled mirror. "Well, Mr. Jesus," he said, "if that happens to be a bomb you are carrying, I will thank you to leave it outside for the duration."

Again, Jesus laughed with delight. "It is no bomb, but you might say a gift, for a man of thought like yourself. The institute of which I speak is The Institute for the Investigation of Faith, housed here in this building where you and Dr. Apple have been debating the existence of God so much enjoyed by one and all. Shall I go on?"

Jesus did not move as long as Bartram studied him in the mirror. At last, Bartram said, "I can offer you nowhere to sit, as you can see this is the only chair. Please continue, though, if for no other reason than that I am dying to know why you have appeared and what this means."

At this invitation, Jesus moved past him, trailing a scent of aftershave and sweat. With his back to him, he busied himself moving scotch and ice aside to set up his contraption on the shelf directly before Bartram. Twice, Jesus glanced at him in the mirror with a bright smile filled with surprisingly white teeth. How old the stranger might be, Bartram had no clue, though he would guess somewhere upwards of seventy, with no top limit. At the same time, he seemed infinitely young, younger than Bartram in his movements and animation. That alone was worth the price of admission.

Speaking to Bartram from the mirror, he gestured toward the machine, which looked like an applause meter, instructing him that it was this contraption which brought him to his dressing room, and which he hoped Dr. Bartram—he did not want to give up the honorific title—would allow him to explain. "I imagine you have heard of the so-called God gene?" When Bartram nodded, furrowing his brow in confusion, Jesus pinched his own lower lip between thumb and forefinger of one hand. "How to explain, when so much has gone into this—so much that would interest a man of your persuasion. Is belief or non-belief a matter of genetic make-up? What do you think?"

Bartram shrugged, eyeing the scotch the other side of the machine.

"What if," Jesus continued, "such things we hitherto considered immaterial substance—I refer to the soul, etcetera—actually come down to material substance, the brain, nerves, so on, do you follow?"

Jesus spun to face Bartram, one hand on the machine. "This we are attempting. We have located this God gene, and everyone has such a thing here." He tapped his temple. "At the same time, we have come to acknowledge that the idea of the gene, of genetic make-up, of the double helix we have come to believe some person at some point in time might have viewed with a powerful microscope, are nothing more than metaphors for something we cannot explain. We scientists at the Institute enjoy a little joke now and again, and sometime refer to this gene as the G-spot. Are you with me, Dr. Bartram?"

Bartram nodded, though to what he was not certain. "Do you recall that admonition, in both the Jewish and Christian testaments, of which you often speak, to make a joyful noise unto the Lord? Such a thing exists in every religion, singing, dancing, chanting, humming, even where there is great attention to silences surrounding us. And we have discovered the reason for this."

Jesus waited long enough that Bartram felt he had to say, "Which is?"

"You ask an excellent question!" Jesus slapped the back of one hand into the palm of the other. "Sound, you see, such as in prayer, or song or rhythmic humming." He closed his eyes and hummed for several minutes, falling into a rocking motion as he did so.

"So, you see what I mean. Sound activates this God gene, or God self, Godhead, and so religions encourage us to activate this G-spot for worship. Once turned on, the individual may return to it for reassurance. If I continued humming several minutes, and you joined in willingly, you might experience mild forms of the ecstatic, which you could repeat at later moments, when you feel high or low, up or down. Do you understand what I am saying?"

Bartram's defenses had broken. He might have laughed out loud if he did not still fear this fellow might be out of his mind and have nothing whatsoever to do with the Institute. "So, what you're telling me is..." Here, Bartram trailed off.

"What I am telling you is this apparatus produces a kind of dog whistle, you see, tuned to the God frequency, the Godhead within, the indwelling spirit. In Christianity, it could be referred to as Holy Ghost, if I am not being blasphemous in any way."

"No offense taken," said Bartram with a wave of his hand that sent the final splash of scotch onto his fingers, which he sucked. "You see, I am not a Christian. I am an atheist."

"Yet, you come from the background of the Christian sect, correct?"

Bartram nodded.

Jesus waved his hand in a rolling circular manner. "So, Holy Spirit—you understand—if I am to turn this dial toward center point, which we scientists playfully refer to as 'Angels We Have Heard on High', where I have made this notch and painted it orange on this otherwise drab machine..." When he tapped at the notch, Bartram noted his long fingernails. "And because we are all the same, all human, we may not hear anything for a while, but we will experience mild ecstasy, our Godhead activated, you see. At least in theory. And, as we know, theory and practice may be quite different. Yet, as they come together, bingo! We have lift-off!"

He laughed with delight at his own effusion. "So, you are the perfect subject on which to try this out, as an avowed and practicing atheist who intelligently and willfully rejects the world of spiritual things you cannot see or measure in an empirical sense. This is the very area in which our experiment will rise or fall, succeed or fail.

"Now, I will leave you alone to try this out yourself. If I remain in the room, I would not, or could not, keep my scientific objectivity. So, I invite you to pull your chair closer and turn the dial toward this notch which I point out a second time. Please, do not go further, as the machine is likely to overheat and create disturbances to you and those in the next rooms, if they have not all gone home, as I believe they have."

Jesus clapped his hands with a beatific smile. "Oh, Dr. Bartram, the effect should be far better than that scotch you have been drinking. But you can tell me about it after. I will give you some time, and here, allow me to help you move your chair closer. I think that is fine, sit down again. You will not need this glass. You will find this instructive, sir. If you experience what we think you will experience. You may recognize that this may well take place in every person with the normal gifts with which we come into this world, even though many of us never explore the regions of mind or spirit of which you may soon become aware."

Jesus patted Bartram's shoulder as he passed, which Bartram took as an encouragement. He heard the door snap shut behind him, though his attention was focused on the apparatus at eye level. He wondered if he should touch the thing, but touch he did. Grasping the dial firmly in the one hand, he held on to it, ascertaining it was a simple metal knob, like so many knobs one has learned to turn in this life. His curiosity got the better of him, and he inched it toward the notch. A third of the way he sat back in his chair, noting he had so far experienced nothing. Except, of course, the dull hum of alcohol revolving through his brain.

He once more sat up in his chair and turned the dial further, though he experienced a bout of laughter at the silly experiment into which he had allowed himself to be drawn. He witnessed again the ridiculous figure of Jesus before him—in imagination—excited beyond reason. What a figure he cut! Of course, he understood he himself had become a figure of fun, even of ridicule—to himself and many others, like Dr. Apple. What a fool! Trying to prove God with scientific theorem and mere language, which, of course, could never reach God, or anything like God. Aristotle had explained this centuries ago.

He heard something now, not exactly a ringing in his ears, perhaps a form of music, high pitched, not irritating in any way. Somewhat pleasant, he had to admit. Maybe if he turned up the volume, he could hear it. So, he turned up the volume, until the point of the dial rested in the slot Jesus pointed out with a click of his nails. Very nice. Delightfully pleasant. It lifted the spirit; it filled him inside, made him idiotically happy. He had not even realized how weighted down by the world he had become, but that dissipated, evaporated into thin air.

He might have approached such a sensation that year he lived by the Pacific, writing his first book. Yes, that had been quite an experience. The book lifted him up and carried him away. Now, he realized what Jesus had spoken of, this mild ecstasy—though it did not seem so mild to him at this moment, which made him realize, intellectually, how depressed he had been every day of his life the past few years. He felt the Holy Spirit inside him, elevating mind, recalling a phrase that had not occurred to him for many years: Music of the Spheres. That's what he heard around him, but was it music, feeling, or pure thought, his mind rising to the best of which it had ever been capable. Tears flowed from his eyes, down his cheeks.

"This is the day the Lord has made," he cried aloud. But as feeling ebbed a bit, moving back toward normalcy, he had a fear he would return to his previous state, in which he had been so deadly unhappy. Naturally, he cranked up the volume, higher, and then higher, but as he did, something began to change. His mood turned on him as forms took shape around him, one dark robed, hooded figure emerging from the closet—he saw it in the mirror. And leaning beside the door, some wicked creature too human not to be cruel, grinning at him.

Something brushed by him, and he saw what in the mirror, the dark shape, the coldness, and three tiny devils on the shelf beneath the mirror, multiplied into six, watching him, laughing, pointing blades and tridents. A thing behind him whispered: "Who the hell do you think you are? Why have you never listened, when I have so much to tell?"

"Bernard," the creature emergent from the closet whispered; the demons cackled it. They saw him; what was worse, he saw them. Had they always been there? He had never seen or heard them except in his nightmares of torment. Had these specters always been there, waiting for him? Had he been protected from them by his unbelief? And, if so, could he now return to it? A voice deep inside his mind—his own this time—spoke loudly—turn the damn thing down.

He struggled to reach a hand to the dial, and as he grasped it felt how hot it had become, burning to the touch, taking skin off his fingertips. "Jesus," he shouted, as rancid smoke emerged from the machine. Jesus ran past him, shouting, "Unplug it, Dr. Bartram."

But as Jesus lay his hands upon the infernal contraption, it cracked open, sending springs and gears, wires of red and blue, bolts and nuts spinning outward, bouncing on the shelf, the floor, knocking solidly on Bartram's skull. "Too late!" Jesus shouted forlornly.

As Bartram watched, the machine melted to a hard, black lump, filling the room with the acrid odor of burning plastic, rubber and metal, and still creatures and shapes and forms did not go away. Not one showed the slightest inclination to cease calling his name. He saw the face of Jesus frozen in a scream he could not hear above the din that clattered on his ears and vibrated on his skin. "Do not answer them," Jesus shouted, though Bartram could barely hear him. "Oh, do not answer them, Dr. Bartram."

But Bartram had sunk into his chair, his mouth and eyes wide in terrible rictus, his fingers fumbling at his face, unable to speak a word to Jesus or answer the demands of the voices now calling to him with increasing urgency. When the Institute's maintenance men found him in this position in the morning, the empty bottle of scotch in his lap, he was taken to a hospital, from there to the morgue, where an autopsy determined that he died of alcohol poisoning.

Stories in newspapers and on television the next few days eschewed any of the more sensational details, identifying his various accomplishments. Gloating satisfaction remained to the shock jocks and bloggers who dragged him over hot coals the next weeks, months, and years, until he was all but forgotten—to everyone but Dr. Ollie Apple, who had his own demons to confront. He felt some responsibility for the death of his old friend Bernard Bartram, even though he still felt the joy of victory in their debate. The Institute, the Press, and the talking heads had given him that much.

But, quite frankly, Bartram had lost interest halfway through taping. Apple knew because he had watched it many times over, long after the distance between the words he spoke and what he felt inside caused him to recognize that he no longer believed in anything. As he believed in nothing, he saw no reason to put an end to his career. His wife and children still required a house, food on their table, clothes on their back, all that living in affluent society demanded. In the short or long run, what difference did it make? He would keep talking until he ran out of words.

The choice had been taken from his hands.

# THE DETECTIVE'S SON

MY FATHER—THERE is a whole world in those two words—never had time for anything but his job. He was always gone, a gaunt figure on the edges of my world, roaming the perimeter with his eye cast anyway but my way. When he disappeared from our house entirely, I was barely aware there had been a divorce as mother and I kept living as we always had. Instead of a dark figure at the door, in the hall, in his chair reading a newspaper, an enormous mug of coffee in one paw, he became a voice on the phone, a Christmas visit from a dissolute and rumpled uncle. Often, I passed him on the street without the slightest nod of recognition.

He smoked. He drank when off duty. He read newspapers. Luckily for him, his work interested him, engaged him completely, or he might have drunk to excess. He was never cruel except in a passive way—he barely knew I existed. I had to learn what I could from whomever I could, from my mother—what she would tell— from colleagues, from the newspapers, from the criminals he put away, and with whom he had lasting relationships. If it is the duty of a son to know his father, to set out on the seas of knowing, I did find a way to contact him at last, in his fiftieth year. I was exactly half his age and bound on my own private researches—into nothing.

Readers who have lived in Arcady any length of time will recognize elements of stories of the Werewolf that haunted our small-town city, frightening us out of our complacency into an emotional and psychological equivalent of a medieval village overnight. It was at this period we finally made contact, over terror in our streets, because I knew his reading habits, and because I am the son of the detective. I have reconstructed in my mind the moment: my father walking to his office in the station, smoking a cigarette in a wind whipping thin snow through the streets the day after Thanksgiving. How he spent the holiday, I have no idea, but I do know he was one of a few people working the very next day. As he once said, crime never sleeps.

It was six in the morning as he paused beside the parking deck and looked around. Up at the corner the light turned green, the walk sign beckoned, but he became aware of eyes on him— like eyes in a dream—but from where? He glanced at the Christian book store across the street, at a window filled with religious items— crosses, bibles, busts of the virgin. I wish I could have been there to see this first hand but am fairly certain my imagining is as good as truth, for father never varied behavior or patterns. He might have wanted to avoid the eyes until he realized they were staring right at him, at chest level, bulging from their sockets, ringed in red.

How unfamiliar things affect us! What did he think when he stared into those eyes? I have recently read that the human response to the grotesque is first one of horror at what makes little or no sense, and then, slowly, the eye defines the most understandable components of what had boggled the imagination. That is a human head, and that a parking meter—comprehensible elements that make a new whole. But what a head! A black face from which the eyes protruded, a blue tongue bulging from her mouth, black hair raised and twisted about her head: an image of horror. Below the ragged throat, it mounted the pole of a parking meter from which the head had been removed weeks earlier by the city, when it installed a computerized system requiring credit cards: something primitive, something of advanced technology.

Superlative detective that he was, my father immediately set about what he must do next: find the rest of her body before the good citizens stumbled on it, and removed that damned head.

He always carried a cell phone in his overcoat and put it to use, calling for "backup", as they say in the quaint terminology of police work. Three patrol cars sped to the scene, blue and red lights swirling, drawing the attention of a crowd of derelicts gathered, those sad people of a town who are always interviewed for television. Then an ambulance—for all the good that would do— some place to stow the various body parts. Arms they found on the concrete floor of the parking deck, still wearing the sleeves of a dark sweater they had worn before disconnection; bare legs, in work shoes, around the corner; and up the hill, a defeated torso leaned against the wall of an alley, wearing only its lamentable underclothes.

My father had seen the woman before, he realized. She had cleaned his office, and those of several neighboring city structures. He knew her name: Gladys Williams. He had reduced the grotesque image to its humble origins and asked himself a question that directed his attention to the holy once again: What devil did such a thing to a simple soul? Gladys Williams had been a thin, hard-working woman with three grown children, a daughter and two sons. She had watched her daughter's children in the day and attended her church three times every week. A God-fearing woman, her daughter said. Who could even think of such a thing, much less do them to a woman who never hurt anyone, never had a mean thought in her head, had nothing for herself except the love of God!

By the following morning, a Saturday, there was no one who did not know of what had happened downtown. Theories spread, as theories will. Sitting at a table in Starbucks, enjoying a cappuccino, I read the story in the paper. My father was quoted several times. People around me speculated out loud, to anyone who listened. *It makes no sense*, a woman said, but a man at the table with her, sipping at his coffee, assured her that drugs were involved. "The only people who would do something like this are drug lords. She must have been working for them—some kind of message."

"But, Frank, she was a cleaning woman, with children and grandchildren."

"I don't care what it says she was—how else could something like this happen?"

A young man from another table, looking up from his laptop: *They left her in the street, in pieces.* A woman at the counter: *You almost have to believe it was animals.* I saw tears in her eyes. *Or part animals*—a fellow trying to buy a coffee drink—*a werewolf.* He grinned; the shop fell silent. The comment had been irreverent too soon. Such jokes could come later, after shock had settled. But it touched a nerve, I could see.

That was when I got the idea to write my first letter to the editor. I am not a fast writer, but I believe I am an effective one. I considered my words carefully, since I would have to sign my name. The paper wouldn't publish under a pseudonym. At the same time a writer worth his salt will be bold enough to write what he has to say and take the consequences. Otherwise, why write in the first place? I jotted notes in the margins of my paper. I went back to my apartment, sat at my laptop and worked on my letter, reading it out loud often. Every time I thought it was finished, I discovered some new issue or problem to confront.

Finally, I was satisfied, no, delighted with my composition. I could imagine its effect. I knew the only reason they would publish my letter was that I had taken the tack of defending the beleaguered victim. I read it out loud once more, and then louder, before sending it to The Voice of the People with the stroke of a key. As easy as that!

There's nothing strange about taking pleasure in your words, nor should there be. Even the most solemn speech must be written by one who knows the language and its usages. Can we imagine an Abraham Lincoln not taking pride in the simple, beautiful words he composed on the back of an envelope for the consecration of the battlefield at Gettysburg? Was the tear in his eye really for the dead? *For score and seven years ago our fathers*...nice start, that!

I went off to work, but I did not forget that letter for a minute. It enlivened my day, it set me apart. I was not this grease monkey changing oil and tires, I was writer of a letter of power, a letter the citizens of our town would read and to which they could not help but react with some kind of emotion, profound agreement or fury, I did not care which. Underlying this high state of being was the simple knowledge that my father would, at morning coffee, come across the letter I had written, and would read it with his own brand of interest, only to find his name inscribed at the end, with the taunt of a Jr. tied to the end.

As I scrubbed grease and oil from my hands and nails that evening in the shower, I had only the remnants of excitement and the beginnings of the niggling question of whether I should have sent it at all. I drank a tumbler of scotch on ice, watched the basketball game on television, fell asleep on the couch. The day's delirium exhausted me. I woke in the night from a dream in which I was pursued through dark and vacant city streets by an enormous werewolf, only his ears above the office buildings, claws clutching corners as he searched me out in silence.

I held my hand out to the light of the television, which I had never switched off, to learn the grisly news that five o'clock in the morning had arrived, and I was awake. As I stepped into gray light of morning, nearly deafened by the chirping and trilling and cawing everywhere, not to mention the barking of a distant dog, I was thinking of that damned letter. Surely, they would not have rushed it into print the very next day—yet it was timely. The people of Arcady, lost in the dreams of severed parts, would wake to the news of the day, looking for explanations.

When I crossed the threshold of Starbucks at six, the room was crowded with early risers scouring the papers. I snatched one from the stack inside the door and hurried to the counter for my cappuccino and a roll. As soon as I was at a tiny round table, I turned the pages back to The Voice of the People and folded it so I could see the letters. My hands trembled and I smoothed the paper, the smell of ink in my head. Relief settled me—not here, not here. And then I saw a headline which said *Terror in Arcady*, a special section set apart for letters about the tragedy in our streets. And there, with true horror, I saw my own letter, and read it once again, rising off the page toward me!

> To the Editor:
> Like everyone in Arcady, I am shocked and dismayed by the horrific events so fresh in our minds. My heart goes out to the family, in the hope that they will find some consolation in their time of grief. What concerns the rest of

us at this juncture is what comes next. Someone must be held responsible.

Surely the death penalty awaits the person who could conceive of and carry out such hideous deeds—regardless of motive, for what decent mind could imagine a reason to justify such bizarre and ugly crimes the enormity of which we have never seen? I have heard wild theories of what happened, on the streets and in coffee shops. Some say she must have had something to do with the drug world. How unfair!

The fact that she was African-American may have allowed some to diminish her worth, but this was a woman of our community, with three grown children of her own, grandchildren to care for when she wasn't working her job. How can we be so heartless as to cast aspersions on her mutilated body? Let us take a moment and have a heart for those who suffer—give her the benefit of any doubts: Judge not lest ye be judged!

No more about the woman who perished; the treatment she received once and for all expiates for any paltry sins that lay heavy in her heart. Such heinous crimes can have no human motive! I hesitate to say I am almost persuaded to side with speculations that some hideous beast prowls our streets at night, monster of our nightmares—a werewolf!

How else can we explain what happened on our streets? And when the monster is captured, let us treat him as the beast he is. Let us offer him a little of that Old Testament justice—an eye for an eye, a tooth for a tooth!

William Furlong Auger, Jr.

Arcady


I read it over, alarmed not so much by the content as by the tone, at something off kilter in the voice, very nearly demented. My anger stirred. How could I be angry at what I had written? Ashamed, I would have understood. I read again as if I had not written those words at all. My anger mounted: what variety of idiot would write such a letter! And then a brilliant, paralyzing flash froze me in my chair. I knew my father was reading the letter at this very moment!

I work for Abel Popescu, who runs a service station that's been in town as long as I can recall, always owned by some new immigrant. Before him a German named Glockner; it still bears the name of Boyle. Abel's a short fellow with curly blond hair and a vague and indeterminate face, by which I mean that it is hard to see what he looks like. When I close my eyes, I see two things: his lips are wet and he has a bump in his nose the size of a knuckle. His eyes are blue, I believe, and squinty. He plays soccer on the German league because I saw him once—a roving goalie in baggy shorts, a cigarette dangling from his mouth. Around the station, he wears what I call a fisherman's sweater with a t-shirt visible beneath, some kind of dark slacks and tie shoes.

"No more letters, Billy boy." He drew his finger back and forth in front of me. "You hear me, Billy? No more letters. You know what's good for you."

I've always had a way with cars. I took a shop class in high school where we worked on teacher's cars for next to nothing, so I had some skills. Abel doesn't exactly like the looks of me so he keeps me on oil changes, simple fixes, and because we have four ports, I'm always busy. I can do a more, but he doesn't trust young Americans to do anything but eat, he says, but at least "you no *negru*." I don't mind, since this is work I do, nothing that I want to do. I get the car up on the rack, drain oil, check fluids and filters, rotate tires. I dip them in water to see where they spit, replace stems, check problems that mean more repairs, rust and ruin of a Northeast Ohio winter, fan belts, nothing any monkey worth his grease can't do—the big stuff he saves for his German giants—they have the knowhow!

Someone told him my father is a detective—that made it worse because he never liked the police but has a sense he ought to keep on their good side. He asked me why I work on cars if "my father is detective". I just shrugged. I pretend I'm a deaf-mute as much as possible. I don't talk about the years I spent trying to get a degree until I got fed up. I took writing classes, and that was what I liked, but no one ever returned the sentiment. People seemed to recoil from what I wrote. They wanted more hearts and flowers. I thought I had a little feeling for the kind of thing people wanted to read outside a classroom, but nothing has transpired yet.

So, I continue on my own, read what I like, write what I want. I send out feelers to agents and editors, but they come back so fast it makes my head spin. I've got pages and pages, so when I hit on this letter to the editor everything came together. Then I had a bad case of regrets. Who am I? What business do I have in Voice of the People? I go to work, spend each day dreaming among car engines, come home with a smell of oil and grease that never goes away. I sit at my laptop and fool around with this or that. I really thought I had something with the letter, but I came down the other side of that experience.

In the next two weeks I didn't write a word, but I did keep track of letters to the editor, looking for any reference to mine—several right away, one an angry woman with an axe to grind, but a couple writers found it sympathetic. All three I snipped and taped in a notebook, but I was disappointed with the visible response. I took note of references to werewolves into the third and fourth weeks after the incident. Something in mine had taken hold with other letter writers. One referred to the werewolf theory of the crime—I highlighted this and included it in my notebook. Any mention of monsters and such I snipped. I began to feel I had planted a seed for a werewolf myth, imagining people all over Arcady sharing my nightmare.

A dull Christmas came and went with no word from my father. I visited mother's grave in Roseville Cemetery. I forgot to mention she was killed in a long skid and spin on the highway during a sudden snowstorm that blinded us for several hours. When I woke next morning, I had no mother, just that stranger in the overcoat, a spyglass to his eye, beat-up fedora shoved down on his head, and the cigarette in his lip that dried his skin into folds of an enormous raisin. He wore dark bags under each eye like badges.

January third my father received a report of another event, same time as before. He sped to the scene, squealed in front of The Islander, a bar on Main Street popular among the young. A tall thin man dressed poorly for the weather—sweatshirt, scarf, fingerless gloves—stood waiting with his back to the doorway, a fledgling beard along his jaw. He thumbed behind as my father got out gawking at the head on a pole from which a torch had been broken. It lay in splinters on the sidewalk, along with a red cap. An intact torch stood at the other side of the door. Blonde hair hung either side of the face, green eyes that bulged, rimmed in the same red as Gladys, and the blue tongue protruding.

"It's Gary Grover," the young man said, and then leaned over and threw up in the gutter, where, it was obvious, he had already left most of the contents of his stomach.

My father was on the phone immediately. Patrol cars fishtailed out front, attracting whatever roamed streets early on a winter morning of the New Year. Ambulances appeared—two this time—a couple unmarked cars, conjured by my father. Gary's legs, torn ragged from the socket, lay in the alley as if still running in white tennis shoes and socks. Arms tossed out back, the torso propped against the wheel of a car in a parking lot, in a red and gray Ohio State sweatshirt, the hood hanging loose. Shortly after, I was in Starbucks for a morning cappuccino when some fool ran in calling out, "The werewolf struck again!"

I don't know what shocked me most, that it had happened again or that he had used the werewolf myth. I would have to write this one in my notebook without a clipping. Everyone in Starbucks—I counted nine including counter workers—knew what he meant. I am embarrassed to mention the excitement I felt. Another letter stirred in my imagination—butterflies danced in my stomach. I took out pen and jotted notes on margins of the newspaper, writing quickly, as if I had to beat some competitor who might usurp the werewolf myth which I had usurped.

107

To the Editor:

The werewolf struck again—chilling words from the mouth of the man who ran into Starbucks early January third. Those gathered inside for morning coffee knew at that moment what he meant. It needed no explanation. As one, we felt a mutual anguish, an awful loss in our community: a young man, a college student with his future before him just the evening before, celebrating his twenty-first birthday with friends, a beer or three to commemorate his coming of age.

Not to be, these words echo in my mind like the raven's cry of Nevermore: not to be, not to be!  Because the monster in our midst determined it: I see him in dreams grown huge, stalking our midnight streets with eyes of fire, a heart of stone.

God help us, words heard in the heart. They run between us like electric impulses through the synapses of a collective mind that is our precious city.

How long till we show up in the street bearing torches like those that burned in front of the tavern where he died—crying out for justice, for the sparing of our young!

William Furlong Auger, Jr.

Arcady

I wasn't laughing; there is such a thing as serious art. Abel Popescu whispered in my ear, "No more letters, Billy-boy." I hit send; it was gone.

I haven't mentioned the photographers. I left them out of the crime scene. They were there, if you want to go back and insert them. Because I've seen the photographs, that's how I know, awful things that lack the slightest glow of romance. It was my father on the phone.

"Son," he said, as if he'd forgotten my name, "if you want to write about this, you'll need to have a better view. You want to see the shots of what you're talking about, I can stop by your place or meet you anywhere you want."

"Where are you now?"

"I'm outside your apartment, in my car."

"I can see you."

"Shall I come up?"

"Come on. I'll make a pot of coffee."

"Never mind the coffee. Have you got scotch?"

"I sure do."

"Well, are you going to let me in or not?"

"I'm coming."

I galloped down the stairs and opened the front door. My father stood there looking in at me. "Long time no see," he said.

I went ahead and let him follow. Once inside, he dropped onto my couch and set a large manila envelope on the coffee table. I brought the bottle and a couple glasses and poured a few fingers of scotch. He never took ice that much I knew, and I wasn't about to put any in mine.

"Sit down here, son."

"My name is Bill, Dad."

"I know, son, I gave it to you."

The crevices in his face had gotten deeper. He smelled like rubber bands. He had the envelope open, spreading large photographs, the size of typing paper, on the table. I sat down beside him. "Over there," he said.

I pulled up the chair and sat across from him.

"All right, Mr. Werewolf, look at these." He tapped the first one. "That belonged to a woman who cleaned my office. I saw her many nights. I talked to her about her children. She was a decent woman. These are her limbs, her torso."

I expected black and white, but they caught the light and shimmered in livid color.

"This young man was celebrating his manhood, top student, International Law. He might look like a surfer but he sure as hell wasn't—not that it matters."

My father studied the pictures for a long time in silence. I don't know why they had no effect on me. They tore at his heart and mind, I could see that.

"You ought to think of retiring, Dad."

"What would I do? Take up golf?"

"I've seen enough, Dad."

"I'm not sure you have, son."

"I'm pretty sure I have, Dad."

"I want you to look a while longer. If you want to move in with me and finish college, I'll pay for it."

"I think I'll pass on that, but thanks."

"I thought I'd make the offer."

"That's awful swell of you."

"I've lost my taste for sarcasm, son, but help yourself."

He gathered up the photographs and shoved them in the envelope. He got up, downed the last of his scotch, and handed me the glass. "You want to write about these people, I want you to think of what you've seen in these photographs."

"I don't suppose you'll let me have them."

"Not a chance."

"I'm glad to see you haven't lost your hat."

"Thank you for the thought."

He took a pack of cigarettes from his coat pocket and shook one out.

"No thanks, not for me. I'd just as soon not look like a prune when I'm your age. I can only wonder what your lungs look like."

"I'm sure they're not a pretty sight."

"Do you still carry a magnifying glass with you, and a great big calabash pipe?" He reached deeper in his pocket and fished out a large magnifying glass, held it out to me. "I find it useful more often than not."

"Why would I want it?"

"Take it. I want you to have it. Consider it a birthday present."

"Gosh, you remembered. You missed by several months, but close enough."

"I have no idea when your birthday is, and why the hell should I? What's there to be so excited about? You're here. You have the same chance as everyone else."

"I thought you were pretty moved by that fellow's twenty-first. You seemed all broken up for him."

"He's dead. You're not. When you're dead, I'll remember the day that you were born."

"So, you think I'll die before you?"

"On the off chance, I should have said. We never know what fate has in store for us."

"It's a regular box of surprises, isn't it?"

"That's the understatement of the year."

"Thanks for stopping by to show me your pictures."

"They're not pictures, son, they're photographs."

"Thank you for stopping by to show me your photographs."

"I thought you might want to see them. In case you did, that's why I came. I only want to help you grow in your chosen profession."

"You might have thought of that a long time ago, when I needed a father to play ball with me."

"You want to play a little catch? I've got some time right now."

"Gosh, I don't have a mitt or a ball."

"We don't need those fancy things. We'll play with a stone, a stick, like the poor kids do. Kick a can through the street together."

"I hate to see you go, Dad. We'll have to do this again sometime."

"Name the time. You've got my number. It's a two-way street."

"Before you go, you got any crime-stoppers for me?"

"Always lock your windows and your doors before the burglar breaks in the glass."

"Thanks for the help."

He touched the brim of his cap.

For a moment, I thought I was going to cry.

"Come here, you oaf." He opened his arms and I moved inside.

"You know I love you, don't you?"

"How am I supposed to know?"

"How many Dads you know can talk to their sons like this?"

"You're the only one, I'm sure."

He turned and trotted down the stairs, whistling 'The High and the Mighty'.

"Don't let the door hit you in the ass on the way out."

"Wouldn't think of it," he said.

I went down and closed the door after him. As soon as I got back up, I realized I still had his magnifying glass in my hand. I tossed it on my dining room table. He probably had another two or three. I sat down at my laptop. Now that I knew my father was reading my letters, I got right to it.

To the Editor:

How do we know the beast will strike again? We know because it is a beast. How difficult to keep up the patina of civilization, so hard to wait for the law to take its course. We sit in our domiciles, awaiting the next strike when we might take to the streets ourselves, forming citizen patrols throughout the night, each night for the next three months. If the beast will show itself, we will know it. If not, we have three months of peace.

I call on the newspaper to advertise the meetings and act as the liaison for these efforts. It would take a few hours each night, a brief deprivation of sleep to prevent the horrors we have seen. Surely there are men and women who will act. Surely, we have the nerve to stand against The Beast!

William Furlong Auger, Jr.

Arcady

I'm a man of habits myself. I couldn't stand a morning without my cappuccino and daily paper. I turned to the last page of the first section, folded back the sheets. There it was, on schedule. I wondered if my father had anything to do with the promptness of publication. The letter gave me chills because it committed me to something I had barely thought through.

If the paper agreed to advertise the meetings, and people showed up, what would I do? Would I have the nerve to lead, to do what I said I would? The paper had my email and my cell phone if they wanted to contact me—what if they did? Would I escape or stand and deliver?

These things I did not know, but all decisions were practically out of my hands. I headed off to work, where Popescue snarled on my way in. "I tell you, no more letter, you hear me say this no more letter?"

"Yeah, I heard."

"Why you no stop, Billy-boy? You no listen to boss man?"

Last I heard we didn't live in Red Russia."

"What you talk Red Russia? I no communist, I hate commie man. American boy no care about the communist, you no come from where I come, you stupid boy, stupid, stupid boy."

"I came here to work. That's all. Now if you'll let me, I'd like to get to it. I see two cars in the bays already. What's the story on them?"

"Blue one, oil change. Check fluid, filters." When he pointed to the car, I noticed he had a bad gash on his hand, bound loosely and improperly with strips of gauze.

"That looks bad," I told him. I grabbed his wrist, but he pulled it away.

"What you do?"

"Let me clean this up, get some anti-bacterial on it. We got some in the First Aid kit. I can get that bandage on there so you won't get it infected."

"You think infected?"

"I can't tell yet, but if it is it's going to swell up something terrible. You won't be able to use the hand for a couple of weeks, probably have to get some stitches."

"You can do this?"

"Sure, I can. Come on in the bathroom."

I took him in, unwrapped the hand, which was oozing blood. I washed it good and dried it lightly with paper towel. He kept sucking air between his teeth. "Hurt," he said.

113

"Nothing like it will hurt if it gets infected." I smeared on the anti-bacterial and wrapped it in a clean bandage, tight enough to be secure and keep it from bleeding for a while.

"Don't hold this down at your side. Let's make a sling. Stick the hand inside your shirt, like Napoleon."

"Ha!" he shouted. "Like Napoleon, with his hand in his coat."

"That's it. Keep it still. Try not to bang it around. In a couple of hours, we'll change the bandage and see what it looks like. If it doesn't get better, you may have to see a doctor."

"That is good. That is good. Thank you, Billy. You pretty good for American boy."

Then his face got very serious. "But no more letter, Billy, you get in plenty trouble."

"I won't get in any trouble, Abel. They're just words."

"Just words, that is good. You very funny, very stupid boy—in my country many people die for words." He pointed his crooked finger at me.

"Hurt you very bad. How you know who doing these things? How you know it not government?"

He shrugged, gesturing widely with his good hand.

"How you know it not bad men want you quiet?"

"This is America. We have free speech, to say what we want without fear of reprisals."

"Ha-ha, I say."

I looked back at the blue car in the port.

"That oil's not going to change itself," I said. "I better get this baby up on the rack."

I'd had enough of debating politics with a foreigner who had no understanding of our system. They had fears and paranoia I couldn't understand. I walked toward the car without looking back. He stood in silence. I could feel his eyes on me as I adjusted the lift under the frame.

I took a break in a couple of hours to check his hand. The bandage was stained with blood, but the wound itself looked better. I washed it, coated it with anti-bacterial cream, and wrapped it.

He breathed heavily while I worked on him.

I did the same before time to leave. I'd come in late, so I was expected to stay later, but I wanted to get out by seven. "We have three cars more," he protested. So, I told him I'd stay to help with those and washed my face and hands to revive myself before I started in again. When I told him they were finished it was probably nine, I didn't know anymore. I was hungry and thirsty. I'd eaten crackers and cheese and a coke for lunch. That didn't do the trick. He and the two Germans were having a beer in the garage with most of the lights turned out.

"Hey Billy," Abel called across the garage as I started to leave. He leaned on the hood of a long black sedan in the first port, holding up what remained of a frosty six pack which looked very good to me. I thought I could down one and still get out before ten, but after I downed the first, they laughed at my speed and pressed another on me. One good drink deserves another. I pulled a cold one out, popped the cap. "Man, that tastes good."

"Ha-ha," Abel said. "He say that taste good." He had tried to imitate my voice and the Germans seemed to get it, but it sounded weird to me.

"Billy," the German named Max said. He brushed salt and pepper hair from his face. I had seen Max and Wolfgang lift a Volkswagen off its front tires. These were big boys, and good mechanics. "Abel tells us you wrote the letters in the paper," Max said.

Wolfgang laughed and said, "You're a pretty good writer, Billy."

"Thank you."

"He try make action," said Abel. "Make the action," he repeated, raising his good fist, but he was walking across the garage toward the door. He closed the last bay door and lowered the window screens while I gulped my beer and gabbed with Max and Wolfgang.

"Abel says you've gone to college."

"I haven't graduated yet. I've thought of going back, but I can't seem to get motivated."

"You must have motivation," said Wolfgang. Abel closed and locked the door to the waiting room and stepped back in the garage, leaning once more on the hood of the dark sedan.

He watched as I set the bottle back in the six-pack and said I had to be going.

"He have to be going," said Abel.

Max nodded, but Wolfgang just crossed his arms on his chest. He had huge forearms.

Abel wrinkled his forehead. "Why you like the communist?"

"Excuse me?"

"Why you like the communist?"

"I don't like the communist."

Max said, "I thought you said he liked communism."

Abel shrugged his shoulders.

"Maybe he not like communist," he said.

They all watched my face carefully.

"Yes or no," Max said. "Do you like communism or capitalism?"

"Well," I said. "I'm open to lots of things. In general, I don't like communism. I mean, I don't think it works, for one thing. The idea that the all-powerful state will give up control to create the agrarian utopia is nothing more than a fantasy."

Wolfgang smiled and nodded. "Very interesting, Billy-boy, you talk good for a stupid American."

They all laughed quietly.

"I guess I better be going."

"What he say?"

Wolfgang cleared his throat. "He said, I guess I better be going."

"Is that right English?"

Max explained that I could have said, I guess I had better be going.

"I guess I had better be going," Abel repeated.

Wolfgang nodded and repeated the sentence, and then Able repeated it and they all laughed at the sound of the sentence.

"Is that communist talking? What you say before when you say wrong?"

"I'm not sure how to respond."

"You think it could be communist talk that before?"

"I don't think communists talk any certain way."

Able waved his finger in the air like a windshield wiper. "You very stupid American," he whispered.

Wolfgang looked closely in Abel's face and said, "You are a very stupid American." Abel watched closely and then repeated the sentence.

"Very good," Max said. He explained it to me, "Sometimes we like to have social talk after we work. My brother and I and Abel, we are from different places but we all understand each other, don't we?"

They nodded. "We also like to hear what Americans think."

I nodded, glanced at my watch. "That sounds good. I'd like to do that sometime, but right now I've got to get home."

Abel smiled, repeating, "That sound good, got to get home."

Max corrected his wording and pronunciation, and Abel repeated it several times.

"I think I learn much talk from Billy-boy," said Abel, and he put his arm around me. I saw Wolfgang reaching for something on the work table, and then I saw it was a syringe.

I backed away, but Abel had a grip I couldn't break. Max helped him and then Wolfgang shoved the needle in my arm, and it seemed very quickly that I slumped to the ground.

When I came to consciousness again, I was trussed like a turkey, my arms tied at my sides with inner tubes, on top of a raised rack. The room was dark except for the glow of a work lamp hung on the rack. I couldn't hear a thing from outside. All of the windows were covered. The three talked quietly as they waited and worked, stopping now and again to take a pull off a beer.

"I think he's awake now," Max said. The others looked up. Abel held a long pole with a sharp knife secured to the end.

"You see, Billy," he said. "We drain you just like oil, so you not make mess in car or all over town. Max and Wolfgang take off arms and legs. By time you not care much what happen, alright?"

"What are you doing," I hissed. I found I could hardly speak, like a dream in which I can't call out. "You can't do this."

"We're only sorry you won't be able to write about this," said Max.

Wolfgang giggled.

"I tell you no more letter," Abel scolded. "Now we stick you in you stomach." He gestured with the pole. "We make werewolf, yes?"

I tried to cry out but couldn't.

"What you think of werewolf?" Abel said, and they all laughed.

"Ah-oooo." Wolfgang raised his head in a howl. Max and Abel joined him.

"You howl like wolf?" Abel said, as he positioned himself under me.

"Ah-ooo," said Abel, with his hands on either side of his mouth.

"You think werewolf?" Abel leaned to get right under me and made an upward thrust that entered at the center of my chest, below the sternum. He held it there a moment and withdrew it with a line of red on the blade. It alarmed me, but more like I was watching a thing that should not happen than experiencing pain and witnessing my death.

Blood drained in the bucket below me like oil. I felt weaker but can't say I felt pain, and it kept coming until it sputtered to only a few drops.

That's when the big fellows went to work, wrenching my arms from sockets and tearing them from my body like wings from a Thanksgiving turkey. My legs took work. I heard them breathing heavily, felt hands on my head, pulling at my ears.

Sadness ate my heart as I watched my limbs and torso loaded in the trunk of the sedan. My blood they poured in a large barrel they covered with a wooden lid. The first port door opened, and they set out in their car to distribute parts into the downtown city streets.

I felt emptied, hollowed out.

I had no idea what came next. I floated through the roof of the shop and saw all the way down Market Street, where their car carried me away. I followed at a good clip, until I was over them, attached to the car like a balloon on a string, moving through the downtown streets until they stopped before the courthouse.

Max carried both legs under one arm, my head under the other as he climbed the long steps. Wolfgang had my torso. Popescue brought up the rear, an arm in either hand. My fury was electric! I attacked, to no effect. They laughed as Max climbed up and set my head atop the rifle of the statue of a soldier on the front lawn of the courthouse.

Wolfgang leaned my torso at the base. I shuddered as they tossed my arms and legs and ran down to the car.

When they drove away, and as the car diminished down the street in the morning gray, I felt forlorn. I sat—you might say sat—on a bench beside a patch of flowers as morning grew. I did not want to look at my scattered body, but it held a fascination I could not resist. Every few minutes I turned back to stare, as if I could not remember.

In the distance, I saw someone coming down the sidewalk in an overcoat. I felt a surge of joy: my father—something would be done!

And though I could not imagine anything that would repair the damage I had suffered, all things seemed possible until I recognized the two who followed him, a bit behind, both persons of no official capacity:  an older African-American woman and a young blonde man, a college boy.

They watched my father's every move and gesture as if it might mean something to their future. I stood as they came up the steps. I felt such awful sympathy for father as he passed by on his way to the old soldier.

How painfully I loved him then—with his hands buried in his overcoat pockets and his head down, as if he never wanted to discover any more of what the world could hold.

# THE ANONYMOUS MAN

I AM A possessor of *one of those faces*. I've heard that phrase applied to someone whose face is frequently mistaken for someone else's. In most cases, this might mean a common arrangement of features easily reconstructed in the mind of a viewer as an acquaintance with similar features. In my case, the quality found its extreme. As a boy, other fellows my age took to speaking with me with great familiarity without introductions. Finding no fault in such behavior, I responded in kind.

Childhood friendships seemed ephemeral enough that I valued this ease of intercourse with strangers. I did not have many close friends, at times none at all. I had no idea at the time that anyone experienced others differently. If a teacher called my name in class, I responded. If she looked for me, I raised my hand. There you are, said the expression on their faces. Of course, mother never mistook me for a sibling, as parents will, because I was the only one there.

I did notice, as I got older, eleven or twelve, that she never looked directly at me, but I thought nothing of it. Her eyes swam behind the lenses of her glasses. I had no father I knew of. Mother never spoke of him. She taught third grade. I would call her a dedicated teacher, as she spent most of her time at school or working on lesson plans or grading papers at home.

I never thought of her as very intelligent because third graders took such a large portion of her time. She was older than parents of other children, and it surprised me when we ran into her students or their parents in public. Children hugged her and parents became so effusive in their delight that she rarely introduced me. I often wondered if I was, in fact, her son. Not in a terribly unhappy way. I felt a bit as if I lived alone in the same house with this woman, as if by some kind of accident. If she hugged or kissed me, it was only in passing, as an afterthought or an obligatory gesture.

At thirteen, my virtual anonymity began to disturb me so much I tried various methods of distinguishing myself. I found it too difficult to be brash, like so many boys in junior high, or to keep up a never-ending string of puns. For a short time, I hit other kids in the arm, in a friendly way, as I had seen other boys do. Finally, I decided that my avenue of individuality or peculiarity would be through excelling at my studies.

I had always done fairly well on reports, but now grades became an obsession. No one objected, but it did not make me feel less invisible. In eighth grade, I heard two boys discussing Halloween costumes. Both decided to go dressed as Superman, a popular comic book hero with his own television show. They also decided to go trick-or-treating together. On that Friday, we would all be allowed to come to school in costume.

I felt such a twinge of envy at their apparent friendship that I decided I too would dress as the man of steel. I felt quite pleased with my decision until later that night, as I sat up reading my history in bed, when it struck me that they might feel resentful if I horned in on their plans. Once I closed the book and turned off the light beside my bed, I mulled the anonymity into which I had fallen, no doubt through my own weakness. My own mother, bland and predictable at home, beloved of one and all at school, had the two identities.

I turned on my light and jumped out of bed, going to my bookshelf where I kept several stacks of comic books, taking out a few examples of Superman, studying images of Clark Kent, who generally wore a blue suit, a white shirt, and a tie, all of which I had in my closet. I lacked only the glasses which he tore off when he became Superman. Pulling on the clothes and a pair of black tie shoes, I rushed to show my mother, still at work at the desk in her bedroom.

"What do you think," I squealed in my excitement. Mother looked at me briefly before going back to her planning. "This is my costume."

"Very nice," she mumbled. "But shouldn't you be in bed?"

"Who do you think I am?"

"A Sunday school boy?" she said, without looking at me.

"Clark Kent!" I waited until I had her attention.

"You need glasses. And doesn't he have blue hair?"

Yes, he did, it occurred to me for the first time.

"I'll get some kind of hair dye. And we can put hair spray on it."

"Excellent," I shouted.

Thursday afternoon, once we got home from school, she dyed my hair dark blue and gave me a pair of black-framed glasses with no prescription, as well as a red and blue slant-striped tie she thought would complete the costume.

"Now you look just like Clark Kent," she told me. "A mild-mannered young man." Her eyes swam, but I thought she was looking at my face and shoulders. She adjusted my tie. "You are a good-looking kid, you know that?"

"Thank you," I said, somewhat taken aback by the compliment.

"Come here," she said. When I came, she put her arms around me gently and gave me a squeeze. "You do know, I'm very proud of you."

Then she went into the kitchen and made chocolate chip cookies. We sat together at the table and ate several with milk. Mother had not said she loved me, but she did say she was proud of me. I assumed that she meant about my good grades at school, and nothing in particular about my person. But, for a moment, I wasn't sure.

When I went back to my bedroom I stood at the window, looking at the moon. Not quite at full, I could see the rough, pitted face looking back down at me, great hollow eyes and mouth open in shock. My life was about to undergo a transformation that would find the world changed, as well as my place in it. I put my costume on a wooden hanger on the closet door, where I could look at it in the moonlight through my window until I fell asleep.

Next morning, I leaped out of bed, put on my suit and glasses, and studied myself at length in a mirror on the bathroom door. I ate my cereal and caught the school bus, filled with students in colorful costumes. As I walked in the classroom, Mrs. Thompson looked at me.

"How handsome you look, Bobby," she said. Three girls in the class, all dressed as cheer leaders, took note. Boys among whom I had been sitting since September now looked at me with what I assumed was wonder and admiration. The two Supermen appeared stunned, as if they had encountered their own alter ego. One of them pointed and said, "Clark Kent!"

I must have beamed as I put my book bag under my desk. Both Supermen told me how cool I looked and invited me to go door-to-door with them next night. All day long, teachers and students complimented me. I had achieved my goal of distinguishing myself simply by wearing a suit, dying my hair blue, and setting glasses on my nose. On the playground, I heard a girl ask a friend who I was, and I heard her say, "He's that brain in Algebra. I think his name is Billy."

If she wanted to think of me as Billy, I had no problem with that. The next evening, trick-or-treating with Chad and Travis was the best night of my anonymous existence to that point. We seemed to have always been friends, on equal footing, laughing at each other's jokes, running or walking in step, comparing notes on girls in our classes. Mother sat on the porch handing out the last candies of the night when I got home.

"There's my handsome young man," she said, dropping candy in my bag. "Wash that dye out of your hair before bed. I had to put your pillowcase through the machine twice."

And, so I did, but disappointment withered my joy on Monday, when I went to school in my yellow and red striped pullover, jeans, high-top sneakers. No one noticed me. No one said hi as I went to my desk. I had once more become anonymous. This continued the next few days, at which time I decided to wear the glasses to school once more. Kids watched me come in and go to my desk as if they just then remembered me.

The girl who had asked about me said, "Hi, Billy." I smiled at her, my face warm from blushing. The boys with whom I had gone out on

Halloween said, "Hey." I nodded to them. I had become normal simply by putting on a pair of glasses—as if in order to be seen I had to wear this mask, as Clark Kent wore glasses to avoid being recognized as Superman.

Even my mother seemed to notice, though she forgot they were not prescription lenses. "I knew you'd need glasses one day, Bobby," she said. "My vision is so bad I can barely make out shapes without them. The doctor says I will be blind in my old age."

Once in high school, I realized I could disappear by taking off the fake glasses, something I utilized more than I like to mention. In public, at the mall or movies, walking down the street, I saw faces light up when they saw mine empty of glasses, often calling me by someone else's name. Once more, I found myself in conversation with strangers who believed me someone they had seen a month, a week, or a few days ago. I adapted to any name, making promises for the absent friend who would have to deal with the consequences.

To this point, entangled in understanding my identity, I had not had a relationship with a woman. The only sex I experienced came at my own hand. Having no father, I am told, offers a young man no model on which to construct mating behavior. I read everything about sex I found, reviewed sufficient images of naked female form so nothing would surprise me, and kept myself prepared for such an experience should it come my way.

The moment came for me at college, freshman year. I had not worn fake glasses since high school in an attempt to locate my real self. I remember one freakishly sunny Friday of the week before Thanksgiving break, when a lovely young woman ran up to me and threw her arms around me, shrieking, "Jerry!"

Adapting more slowly than usual, I wrapped her gently in my arms. "Now, who are you?" I asked sincerely.

She responded by giggling and slapping my arm. Her red hair sparkled in the sunlight. Her green eyes fairly glowed against her pale skin, a girl of no more than nineteen. "Shut up, you!" she said. "I'm so glad you came. Are you already out for Thanksgiving break?"

She didn't wait for an answer but took my hand and together we ran to her apartment, one she shared with a roommate not at home that day. I found a Freshman Composition essay on the table while she ran to throw our coats on her bed. Her name was Sally Cummings—I will never forget it—and she had wonderful parents who 'shined' their approval on her. She got a B minus on the paper. From Sally I learned the true nature of kissing with lips and tongue and teeth.

"Oh, Jerry," she whispered.

Gasping for air, tormented by guilt, I told her I had to get back to school for an exam that evening, but I just had to see her. "You have to drive all the way back to Columbus?" Evidently, Jerry attended Ohio State, three hours away on a good day.

"A midterm," I whispered.

"Then you better get, Mister," she said. "You'll pick me up for Thanksgiving?"

I promised, we kissed, long and luxurious, and I fled.

I felt awful I allowed her to believe I was Jerry, but my mind and my body throbbed with desire. I ran back to my dormitory at top speed, and as dusk fell, I stood at my window, looking out at a pale white, thin crescent of moon that had no face, no face at all.

I considered going home early, but I actually had an exam in a Tuesday class. I studied to drive her from mind. On my way back from classes on Monday, I kept my head down. I had gone back to wearing the glasses, and when I passed her on the path, talking on her cell phone, she glanced at me without recognition. I heard her say, "What do you mean, 'What exam?'"

She looked more beautiful than I remembered, but troubled. I rushed back to my room, threw myself on my bed, and beat my pillow to death. The shame I endured was knowledge I had allowed Sally to believe I was her dear Jerry—a gross imposition on her emotions. I allowed her to lavish affections on me intended for him. I am relieved I took flight before indulgence turned to something more serious—from which neither of us could recover.

If I had gently pushed her away as soon as she made her mistake and told her I just had 'one of those faces', surely she would have realized I was not who she imagined. If not, I could have inquired about details of Jerry's life and assured her they did not apply to me until my face re-formed before her eyes. If I carried glasses, I could have put them on and dispelled all doubt. Her temporary embarrassment would have been a source of nothing more than nervous laughter. We could have waved at each other in passing without shame.

Had Sally known I was not Jerry she would have despised me though I fell in love with her. I have been through this every way, and it has made any attempt to establish a relationship precarious at the start. I am not sure of myself. I proceed carefully, as any man should.

Still, I cannot regret holding her in my arms for an hour one sunny day in November long ago. I lost my innocence, if I ever had any. I understood that what came between me and my own proclivities was nothing more than the mask provided by a pair of glasses. When I tore them off, I became invisible, or only partially visible—a form on which to build a person.

I made my way through the college years mildly ashamed of myself, thus appearing humble to the point of clinical shyness. This drew a shy young woman to me in due course, and we talked and shared our favorite everything: color, book, political party, and so on. I do believe we fell in love in the common way. She often tried to think who I reminded her of, a movie star, a former teacher, and so on. I laughed when she thought she had come up with the right name, a new identity, and every time I told her I just had one of those faces.

She did come to know the face with which I came into this world, and I felt pleased she knew my face without the mask. For this I loved her. We went to parks in our region, camping in the natural world where I felt no urgency to be identified by anyone. One night, after sharing a bottle of merlot, I dared her to walk to the very edge of a precipice so I could attempt to take a photograph of her silhouetted against a startling large and orange moon just then rising up the sky. I got as close as I could, and when I could see her clearly in the camera, I saw her troubled eyes searching for me in the dark. She said my name plaintively, a voice tinged with fear.

In that instant a blind fury took hold of me. I rushed at her, hands before me, giving her a push that sent her tumbling clumsily backward until I relented as quickly, grasping a hand before she fell. "What are you doing?" she shrieked. She claimed to have heard a sound behind me, like a bear coming through the trees, which seemed ridiculous to me, and I told her so. I had seen her eyes go blank and searching. I had seen that look before.

Only later did I find her explanation plausible, but by that time she could not look at me directly without fear in her eyes. "I thought I knew you," she told me. By this I knew she had loved me and now did not. I wished her nothing but happiness, stifled my grief, said good-bye. During our time together, we tried to conceive a child, but nothing came of it. I sometimes wondered if we had managed to have a child, would that have kept us together? When I dreamed of the non-existent child, it had no face. I woke trembling, resolving never to father a child for fear he would be like me.

An internal sadness wormed its way into my heart. I considered suicide often, but paradoxically drew strength from these episodes. It may sound strange, but what enlivened me at last was the discovery of a resolve to live my life that drew me back at the final moment. The pills before me on the table, I swept into the trash. The gun that spent several minutes on my tongue, I hid in a drawer. I wanted to live. My insurance career was hateful to me, but for a long time I had no gumption to leave it behind. It paid bills, purchased car and condominium, an occasional night with a woman I reminded of her first boyfriend.

Knowing I would not kill myself, I resolved to live as I wished. I had significant savings by this time, augmented by the sale of my condominium, and began driving around the country, sleeping in the car, staying at cheap hotels, enjoying strange women who believed me someone else, until my funds became depleted. With my gun, I relieved a few chance passersby of their wallets. This sad truth I share with you because I know you will tell no one. Who listens to the moon, whose borrowed light reveals a blind face that reflects my own?

This stale, repetitive, depressing, method of living reminded me daily that I had no face. I began wearing glasses once more, made acquaintances I retained for a while, settling in a small, beautiful town in the Northwest. I took a job at a restaurant, as a waiter, and had no problems until the tedium of this life wore me away to nothing. I lost a great deal of weight, to the point where I could feel my bones if I sat in a wooden chair.

When I realized I was fading out of existence, I became alarmed, quit my job, threw my glasses in the trash can, traveled East, through mountains, holding up several banks without the slightest fear of discovery. I sold my faithful car, took a train to Chicago, where I thought I might live in anonymity if I restrained myself. I took a hotel room and stayed several weeks. I was able to eat again, but found the thought of food repulsive, pain my only emotion—psychological and physical pain I attributed to the deadly loneliness. I had two options: take my life or find a way to live with others. I remembered my mother, who had been kind, if neglectful.

I gathered all my cash in a utility belt I purchased at an Army-Navy store and took the bus to my home town, Akron, the small city where I grew up, and a cab from the station to the little house, so much smaller than it seemed so many years ago. When I knocked at the door, I heard a shuffling inside before the door opened a crack. A chain held it from opening wider.

"Who's there?" she said, her voice so familiar I couldn't make it fit the face before me, the wide-open blank eyes, so light blue as to be translucent. It was then I realized ten years had passed since I last saw her.

"It's me, Bobby," I said. "I came back to see how you are."

She listened and thought a while before closing the door to unlatch it and open it wide again. "Is it really you?" she said.

"Yes, it is. I've come home to see you."

"I wish I could see you clearly. I imagine you look as you did as a boy."

She opened her arms and I walked into them. "I'm so glad to hear your voice, Bobby. Come in, but forgive the condition of the house." She laughed drily. "I have someone come in every week. I don't know what she does, but I pay her for it."

How strange to stand in my childhood home, in the dark hall, looking at my frail mother. I knew even then I had come home to stay. Mother needed me, as no one else did. I told her little of my life after my wife and I separated. I spared her the awful details that might have broken her heart, telling her only that I had sold a business on the West Coast to return home.

She did not press for more, but I arrived a little late. The cancer that would take her life had settled in her bones. I took care of her assiduously, enrolled in classes at the university, and finished my teaching credential a few months after I buried her. I have lived in the house I grew up in ever since, thankful to have found a job teaching near enough to walk.

Like mother, I became the slender, spectacled, and harmless grade school teacher in my infallible blue suit, re-establishing acquaintance with those who remembered me from school but never taking off my glasses, which I actually need now. In my bathroom mirror, I see a face I do not recognize, reminding me of no one. When I look at the moon, I see nothing but an indifferent rock in the night sky. And when I lay down in bed, I am myself at last, containing all I have ever done and been. I sleep soundly, without regret, in the hope that as life draws to a close, as days, months, and years slide past, if I am fortunate, I will never hurt, or love, or hate another human being in this world again, until my face fades from the last memory.

# I AM CALLED MYSTERY

LENA WALKED INTO the living room, tearing brown paper off a book-shaped package she found on her front porch, down to a more festive shiny blue with silver zig-zags. When she sank in the big red chair, she felt like she was on a boat in a foaming sea. Her mother had gotten rid of all the other furniture in the room before the boating accident, when she planned to redecorate in a completely different palate, but they had to have something to sit in.

Lena turned on the lamp on the black-lacquer table beside the chair, opened the small envelope, and removed a card with a hand-drawn cat on the front. Her sister's work, it wore a blue scarf and knit cap. She read the note carefully, alert for the hidden messages they once left for each other. *Lena, it's so easy to remember your birthday, ha-ha. Happy birthday to us! The author of this book is the fella I told you about, my very own dream boat. I hear it's good though I haven't read it myself, who has time? He's off on a reading tour now, so tell me all about it—before he gets back! Love you buckets, Tina.*

Tina says she lives in Washington, on the Puget Sound, and tells her sister how beautiful it is, that she should come live there if she can part with their mother's house. She tells her they have a small boat with a motor, and last time she went fishing with her beau, an orca emerged nearby, dove and disappeared. It was glorious. Their delight and amazement subsumed the fear they later realized they should have felt. The Killer Whale could have capsized the boat!

The story terrified her. How Tina could think she would find this interesting so soon after the catastrophic experience on Lake Michigan, she cannot fathom. As for the invitation to move to Seattle, she can't imagine leaving the only home she has known, the home in which she hopes to recover her lost past—hers by deed and inheritance. Tina had been alienated from their mother and, consequently, Lena, for the last ten years, since they were seventeen.

The black cat she called Mystery jumped up beside her, purring and blinking her yellow-green eyes. Lena set the card and torn envelope on the stand and placed an index finger under the paper and lifted, separating the tape so she wouldn't tear the paper. She lay the wrapping in the floor, still retaining the shape of the book. She had removed the book without looking at it. The dust jacket was red, she now saw, a white staircase floating off-center.

The edges of the staircase had been drawn with broken lines, to indicate it might not be substantial. The title in dark brown cut into the image: *Imaginary Staircase*. In the bottom right corner, also in brown: *Brandon Curtis*. She turned it over to look at the photo of the dream boat, a dark-toned man with lines down either side of his mouth and a dark furrow across his forehead, not the sort she would have called *fella*. Forbidding.

His hair was dark, a little gray over the shapely ears, his eyes penetrating pale blue, eyes that scared the fragile Lena. She, her mother, and sister, all had dark brown eyes to match their hair, faces more round than his. She didn't want to look at him, so she turned the book over. The staircase seemed to float, tilted, off-kilter, like the staircase in a dream, though her dreams have nothing floating, except for her, and then infrequently. She woke from a dream that took place in the room where she sat. She rose from the red chair, floated to the ceiling, bumped gently against it, remaining there for the duration of the dream.

Had she met the man on the back cover but couldn't remember him because it came before the accident? When they pulled her from the oily water, she was so cold, and she could not remember what put her there. When they told her that her mother died, she could barely remember her face. In the photograph of her mother, she and Tina stood on either side. She recognized her sister because she was in the room, right beside the nurse. She said, "This is you." But she didn't know where to point in the photograph, and she did not remember Tina was her sister until she saw her own face in the white frame of a hand mirror. The tall red-haired nurse had a face full of pity and green eyes, greener than Mystery's eyes.

Since then, she has kept the photograph with her. She laminated it and wore it around her neck on a length of red yarn. If she went out, she put it in her purse. When she went to bed, she set it on her bedside table. She wanted to look at it first thing in the morning. In the shower, she hung it on the mirror.

When she opened the book and looked down a table of contents, she discovered it was not a novel or not like any novel she had read. Titles might refer to short stories, but she did not understand what they meant, how they might relate to one another. She saw the name Jessica repeated several times, evidently a girl he knew or imagined. She could not make sense of the book, but it would not be fair to set a gift aside so lightly. Her memory and concentration left something to be desired. She forced herself, out of consideration for Tina, to open it and read the first story, "Blind Girl Wakes in the Dark":

> That morning, before first light, Jessica sat in bed, a tablet on her knees, writing thoughts with which she had awakened. One thought came fast on another when a small green snake emerged from a vent near the baseboard, no more than a yard from where she sat. She finished her last thought before she could take a break long enough to realize what she had seen.
>
> She searched the length of the baseboard. Where had it gone in so brief a time? Under her bed?
>
> She climbed out of bed and kneeled on the cool floorboards to put her head beneath it.
>
> The snake could have been hiding in the sheets and comforter dangling on the other side, so she pushed herself under the bed to rustle the bedclothes.
>
> The door creaked open. Her mother said her name from the open doorway. She repeated her name with confusion, and then she closed the door.

Jessica stood, brushed the front of her nightgown, and sat back on her bed, taking up her tablet and pen. She heard doors opening and closing in the hallway.

"Jessica," her mother said. "Where were you?"

"What do you mean?"

"I just stepped in a moment ago and you weren't here."

"I've been here all morning."

"Well, perhaps I'm losing my mind."

"That would be a shame."

"What are you writing?"

"I had a dream."

Jessica tapped the pen against her chin.

"I was in a strange place and a man I did not know stood waiting."

"What was this place like?"

"Blank. White. Nothing."

"Go on."

"He had a spoon in one hand."

"Perhaps you interrupted him at dinner?"

"He held the spoon against my cheek, cool and smooth."

"Your grandmother had beautiful silver. She set it out every Sunday. How we had to polish it!"

"And something else."

"Oh?"

"He set the tip of the spoon at the corner of my eye and gently pried it from the socket."

"My word!"

"The eye fell on the floor and rolled about. I saw myself from the floor, where the eye lay looking back at me."

"That is strange."

"I covered the empty socket with one hand."

"What were you wearing?"

"Pale yellow, something delicate. He set the tip of the spoon at the corner of my other eye, and do you know what I thought?"

"That he would pry the other eye?

"And that's just what he did."

"For heaven's sake!"

"Now I could see myself and the man quite clearly. Now that Both eyes lay on the ground."

"What did you do?"

"Until this moment, I had not noticed the man had no eyes himself. He was completely normal, except with no eyes."

"What did he look like?"

"Any man, in a dinner jacket and tie. A small bow tie at his neck and dark slacks. But no shoes. I remember his toes against the white floor."

"No shoes?"

"He kneeled before me. I thought he might propose, but he felt along the floor, closer and closer."

"What do you mean closer?"

"I saw all this from the floor, where my eyes had fallen."

"My goodness. What happened next? He didn't..."

"He picked up my eyes and set them in his empty sockets. I could barely see, his thumb and one finger covered the eyes."

"Did that hurt?"

"Not once he had the eyes pushed in his face. I saw the girl in the diaphanous gown."

"The yellow one?"

"Pale yellow. She too had no eyes and held her hands out like a blind woman."

"Poor thing!"

"But I could see perfectly well."

"From the young man's eyes?"

"My eyes saw whatever he directed them toward."

"Gracious. What did it feel like to be a man?"

"No difference."

"None at all?"

"Except, now that I think of it, tender."

"Painful?"

"Tender feelings, fear of the eyeless woman as she reached about, hoping to find...something."

134

"This is what you have been writing?"

"And other things."

"I couldn't have thought of anything else, after such a dream."

"My mind wandered. I saw a snake."

"A snake?"

"Coming through the vent, along the baseboard, and then it disappeared."

"Where did it go?"

"I thought it might have gone under my bed. I rustled the bedclothes a bit, but nothing emerged."

Jessica felt her mother's arms closing about her but could not hear her words as the huge green head came through the door. She did not alert her mother in fear of scaring her, and could not find her voice at any rate, not even when the mouth closed quietly around them and the dark surrounded her.

This too was like a dream, and the only staircase Lena could imagine was outside Jessica's bedroom, leading downstairs, though it had not been mentioned. It was a terrifying staircase for Jessica, because she was blind. Lena looked into the large white fireplace to keep the room from spinning. Her mother removed the andirons, wood basket, and the grille that once held burning logs. Workman had cleaned and scrubbed it, intending to repaint or redesign the interior and the frame. She closed the book and set it on the side table, beside the lamp, which she switched off.

Plenty of light poured through the bare windows. Then she saw a shadow move between the trees, coming up the walk. A man in a dark trench coat and hat disappeared behind the wall, and she heard the clanging of the door knocker. She sat quietly, hoping it would not be repeated, but the sound broke through the house again, clear and sharp. Then she heard the man's deep voice, calling, "Lena?"

She imagined him outside the door in his black coat and hat, saw his pale blue eyes. When the clanging repeated, she stood up in alarm, and could not stop herself from going to the door, pressing her ear against the wood. When she did, he called, "Lena," right through the door.

"Who is it?" she said faintly.

"Is that you, Lena?"

"Who are you?"

"Bradley Curtis. I'm a friend of your sister, Tina."

"I have your book. Tina sent it for my birthday."

"Good Lord, it's your birthday? Well, happy birthday! I'll have to call your sister and tell her happy birthday as well. Maybe you can help me pick out a gift?"

The pause grew longer, and when she heard a rapping on the long living room window, she gasped. She took a step into the living room and looked through the window. He stood outside waving at her, but not smiling. "Are you all right?" he shouted. This was more difficult to hear than when her ear had been at the door.

"Go away," she whispered.

"I can't hear you."

"What do you want?" She stepped back in the foyer. He moved so he could attempt to see her, but it was darker in the foyer, and then he disappeared. She felt a little relief but she jumped when she heard a thin, metallic screech. He had lifted the mail slot.

"I'm on a reading tour and thought I should stop to say hello. I'm quite close to Tina, as you know. I'm perfectly harmless. I know about the accident. Sorry about your mother. Tragic."

She leaned down so she could see his mouth at the slot.

"No problem. Perfectly understandable. I'll be on my way then, hope to see you another time. I should have called."

The slot clinked, and she listened to hear steps walking away. She stood waiting for the sound of his car. Several minutes passed in silence, then Lena's phone rang. She went through the dining room and into the kitchen to answer it. "Hello?"

"This is Bradley Curtis, as I said before. Sorry I alarmed you. I assure you, my intentions are honorable, even if my performance is awkward." He laughed softly. "Is there a better time to stop by, or perhaps you would come to my reading at the Barking Squid

Bookstore? There won't be more than two or three people, and you'd bolster the crowd."

"Hi, Bradley," she said. "It was good to meet you. I'm not feeling well at this time, and I wouldn't like you to catch what I've got."

"Oh, dear. I hope it's not too bad. Are you by yourself here? Do you need anything? I'd be glad to fetch something from the drug store or the grocers."

"No, thank you. I have all the medication I need."

"Well, that's fine, then. I'll just be on my way. At least I got to talk to you. When I call Tina, to wish her happy birthday, I'll tell her we spoke. Should I suggest that she call?"

"That's not necessary. But you might think about garnets."

"Garnets?"

"There's a jeweler in town that has garnets with antique-looking settings. I think she would like those. For her birthday."

"Wonderful. Thanks so much. I'll keep my eye open for the jewelry store. Tina's going to chew me out for not calling first so can I just tell her I called to say hello with no mention of the rest?"

She shrieked then, because she saw him looking through the back door.

"Get away," she said. "Get away, or I'll call the police."

He waved and smiled. "No need. I just wanted a good look. It's remarkable. You two are mirror images. If I saw you on the street, I'd swear it was her."

He was perhaps a foot taller than her, his face surprisingly animated. He took his hat off and bowed a little. "I'll call again, if it's all right, from a more distant location."

Then he clicked off and disappeared around the house.

Now she waited in the kitchen several minutes, then crept through the dining room into the foyer, to the front door. She turned the doorknob stealthily, pulled the door open a bit. She shrieked to see him on the porch, looking down into her face, and slammed the door shut.

"I wanted to give you a flyer for tonight," he called. A gold paper came through the mail slot. "I had them in the car. I've written my phone on it as well, in case you want to call."

She picked it off the floor, a simple photocopied sheet that announced his reading at The Barking Squid Bookstore tonight at 7:30. He had written his name and number on it as well, in blue ink, with a quickly drawn smile with two wide eyes and a longish nose beneath it. It looked plain enough to be true, so she sighed and opened the door.

"It would be wrong to turn you away," she said.

"I'm so pleased," he said. His smile looked enormous and over-happy. It made her take a step back. He followed her into the living room and looked around for a chair.

"You'll have to bring a chair from the dining room, or we could go back here and sit in the sun porch."

"The sun porch sounds good," he said. "I see you have a garden out back."

"My mother's plot, gone to ruin in the past couple of months."

"So sorry to hear what happened on the Lake, an explosion of some kind?"

"That's what they told me. The engine or something."

"You don't suspect sabotage?"

Lena sat in a hanging wicker seat in the sun porch, and he sat on the love seat. Unlike the living room, the sun porch was furnished in an outdoor motif, plants hanging over windows and skinny trees standing about, one that looked like a palm. "Love the rug," he said.

"Lebanese," she explained.

"I saw my book on the table in there, beside the red chair. You must have just gotten it. I noticed Tina's wrapping paper. Otherwise, it's pretty vacant in there."

"Mother got rid of everything. She had decorators measuring and photographing and then she died. I haven't had the heart to go on, and I like sitting in that old room with nothing but the chair. And here she is!"

"Your mother?" He looked toward the doorway suddenly. The cat, who had made herself scarce, appeared in the doorway.

"And who is this?" he said to the cat.

"I am called Mystery," she said, as if she were the cat.

"Well, Mystery, you are indeed a beautiful creature." She walked along the edge of the room opposite Brandon and jumped in the hanging chair with Lena. "May I have a look at what you have around your neck?"

Lena took the red yarn over her head and handed it to him. He had to reach to take it, and sat on the edge of the love seat studying it. "Except for your mother's age, the three of you could be clones."

"I'm on the right," she said. "That's Tina on the left."

"I wouldn't have known." He handed it back to her. She pulled it back over her neck and settled in with her hands in her lap. "It's remarkable you've had so little to do with Tina."

"As I understand it, she's had little to do with us. She brought me this photograph in the hospital. We were sixteen in the photo. I really don't remember her much, but I feel I know her, because we look so much alike."

"They say twins often have a preternatural connection, even when separated."

"I don't feel anything. We just look alike."

"Maybe there's more to it. Maybe you have to tune in to it." He moved his hands as if he was shaking an imaginary gift. Lena watched them until he stopped. He crossed his arms and sat back. "I can see you've been hurt," he said.

"I was knocked unconscious and pulled out of the water when I had already drowned."

He shook his head. "Sounds life altering."

"I don't remember everything, but I miss my mother. We did everything together. Living out here by the Lake, we had our own world. I think of her as my twin."

Lena rocked her chair as she spoke. "You've heard of phantom limbs. That's how I feel about my mother."

"And your sister?"

She shook her head. "Nothing. She's not there, except intellectually. It doesn't hurt."

"But maybe there's something to explore, the possibility of a new relationship opening up between you. She has nothing but good feelings about you."

"She doesn't know me."

They sat in silence a few minutes while the cat cleaned her rear legs. "Quite a cat," he said. "Look how she stares at me."

Lena nodded.

"How did you come up with the name Mystery?"

"I couldn't remember her name."

"Do you ever call her Misty, or Mistry?"

"Oh, sometimes I call her Mother, but I usually don't call her anything. She doesn't require it. I don't often hear my own name, and I don't seem to need it either."

"It's a nice name, Lena. You're quite a mystery."

She let the cat crawl on her lap and stroked the length of her body. "Her name is Mystery, and this is her body, but where is the true Mystery? What is she, really? She does like to have her body stroked, because it feels good to her, and I like to pet her. Sometimes I think petting her has the effect of reminding her where she is, that she's here, in this space. That's comforting, but I feel she is so much more than that."

"Hemingway said a story is like an iceberg, most of it underwater, unseen. Maybe that's what being alive is like."

She nodded, but tears came to her eyes.

"Did I say something that pained you?"

"I know I should know that name, Hemingway. But I don't know who he is."

"A writer, dead now. He killed himself."

"I'm sorry."

"This happened years ago, in 1961. He taught American writers who they are."

"That sounds important. I'm going to want to know more about him. Will you write his name down before you go?"

"I'll send you a novel of his, if I may."

It had begun to rain outside, and the light had grown dim. "You have a reading tonight, at a bookstore?"

"I have half a mind to blow it off."

"It's been nice talking to you, but I think this has been enough for me in one sitting. You have been very sweet to come and see me. I appreciate the time you took." She stood up and he looked at her a moment quizzically.

"Is this it, then?" he said.

"No," she said. "I have something for you. I'll be right back."

"Shall I come?"

"No, please. Wait here."

Lena walked swiftly through the living room, into the foyer, hesitating at the bottom of the stairs with one hand atop the newel. The dark at the top of the stairs looked forbidding. She had slept in the sun porch several nights, on the love seat where Brandon sat. Here, she felt her mother most. She had to be able to walk up the stairs of her own house. She rarely felt up to it, but she took each step with determination as she moved into the dark.

At the top of the stairs she felt along the wall for the light switch. When she found it, she held it in her fingers a moment before she flipped it. As much as she feared the dark of the hall, she hated to dispel it, as if dispelling the spirit of her mother.

She walked to the end of the hall, to the door of the room in which her mother had slept and opened it carefully. She felt her watching as she went to the dresser. Avoiding the mirror, Lena opened the jewelry box, lifted the top shelf, and felt through her mother's bracelets for one she knew by feel, removed it, and closed the box. Then she looked at herself in the mirror, and saw what she dreaded, her mother watching her.

"For Tina," she said, "because she liked it when we were girls."

She hurried out, closed the door behind her, and hurried down the stairs. He stood waiting in the living room, holding his book. "I hope you don't mind, but I signed it for you." He turned and set it on the chair.

"I have something for you," she said, "for my sister's birthday. Put out your hand."

He opened his hand to her, and she held his wrist as she placed the bracelet in it.

He stretched it out on his palm and studied it a few minutes. "It's beautiful," he said. "Is it garnets? I thought they were always red, like pomegranate seeds. Are they orange?"

141

"Tina loved to wear it. That was something I remembered, when you said you had to get something for her birthday. She loved that bracelet. I hope she still does."

"I'm sure she will," he said. "I feel I should say I can't accept this, but it's for Tina. So, I can't say anything but thank you, for her. Kahlil Gibran tells us to rise on the wings of the gift with the giver, and so I will, and I know Tina will be thrilled."

"You don't want to be late for your event."

"You won't consider coming?"

She shook her head. "Thank you. This has been very special for me. I am so glad that you came. That you persisted." Mystery meowed loudly behind him. He looked back and then went to the door. When she followed a few paces behind, he stopped at the door.

"I hope you will someday feel we are part of your family. Tina wants that, and now I do. You have touched my soul."

She lowered her head as he shut the door behind him. She waited until she heard his car starting at the top of the yard, beyond the trees, and then she went to the red chair, turned on the light, and picked up the book. She opened the cover, to where he had written, "This for my dear love's sister, who I hope one day will be my own." Under this, his signature and the smiling face he had drawn on the flyer as well.

Brandon Curtis slid his key card through the slot on the door of room 362, opened the door and stuck his long head inside. "Are you indecent?"

Tina lay propped up in bed in a pair of orange pajamas with catheads all over them. Her long, dark hair was tied back in a ponytail. He gave her a big smile as he hung his damp coat and set his hat and a plastic bag from the bookseller on a shelf in the closet. Her dark eyes followed as he came and sat on the foot of the bed, gave one of her feet a squeeze, leaned down and bit her toes.

"Ow!" she said, without moving her foot. She smiled when he bit the toes of her other foot. "Cut it out. Tell me what happened." She turned off the television, rearranged the pillows so she could sit up straighter, and waited.

"Well," he said. His blue eyes darted back and forth.

"Just tell me," she said.

She leaned toward him and to smack his head, but he grabbed her hand and started biting while she slapped at him with the other. He lurched, grabbing her small shoulders, and buried his face in her breasts until she laughed hysterically. He scooted up beside her and stole one of her pillows to prop himself up beside her.

"So?" she said.

"Well," he said. He turned on his side and looked at her face. "It was freaky, freaky, and freaky."

"Really?"

"She looks exactly like you. I mean exactly. Her hair is short, and she has a major stick up her ass, but it was you, done strange."

"Like how, strange?"

"She wouldn't open the door strange. I talked through the mail slot first, and then on the phone, while I watched through the back door. I was persistent, and thus she let the handsome stranger in her house at last."

"And..."

"And," he said, digging in his pocket. "Here is proof this was not a dream."

Brandon dangled the garnet bracelet before her. She took it immediately and put it on and held her wrist up to look at it.

"What do you think of your birthday present? From your dear sister."

"Mother let me wear it a few times. It made me feel dazzling. I tried to take it when I left, but that led to a huge confrontation, and I just left. It's mine, by natural feeling." They watched her turn her wrist. "And they make me feel almost peaceful inside."

"I had to work hard for them," he said. "I had to charm your lovely sister."

"Did you?" she asked, still watching the bracelet. "Don't hold me in suspense, you bastard."

He settled back, closed his eyes. "I believe I did. I think she might have been reluctant to let me in because she knew she was so easily charmed."

"She had your book?"

"She had unwrapped and read a bit of it. Thanks to the brilliant stroke with the flyer, she thinks I am now reading from it at The Petulant Frog."

"So, a change of plans?" Tina looked up at him, her eyes scorching him.

"The resemblance is uncanny," he said.

"So, at least you saw the house."

"The lot is spectacular, wooded. I saw the stream running at the back, beyond a funky garden plot. The interior in good shape, though the living room is furnished with one red chair and a lamp. Your mother removed everything, as part of a redecorating scheme. The sun porch, where we sat, again, spectacular. Kitchen, immense. Dining room, unused, stately. Formal foyer, ridiculous with an old-fashioned chandelier. Gorgeous rugs, dining room, sun porch, and both Lebanese. I didn't see the second floor."

"I'm thankful for that."

"Yes, well, time was a factor. You expected me back before morning."

She struck him with one small fist, and he laughed. "God, it was tempting. She looks so much like you, the only difference her hair. And you know how crazy I am about you, darling."

"I'll get my hair cut short, if you'll show me how she had it."

"Simple page boy, bangs. A little bit of a flapper. Quieter, perhaps. If I were making the movie, I'd film this scene first. Then, cut your hair and have you play both roles."

"Oh, really? And what would the later scenes look like?"

"Brandon and Tina, happily in your mother's house. I see a lovely wedding in the back yard, a summer wedding, the garden flourishing, enormous sunflowers nodding approval. And me writing my play on the sun porch, now my study, as you redecorate the entire house on the proceeds of my first novel, which will have been published to acclaim and untold riches."

"Once I am Lena, you won't need to make a killing right away. I'm sure there's enough in the bank, or invested, to keep the old place going."

"A sweet thought. Still, I do plan on getting rich on my writing."

"Another sweet thought."

"A sweet life awaits the parting of a curtain."

"I can't wait, Brandy. I won't."

Brandon gathered her in his arms, and they lay quietly dreaming until he sat on the edge of the bed, picked up the phone, made the call. "Brandon Curtis here again, your sister's friend. I do hope you don't mind my calling a second time tonight. I finished the reading, and picked up a book for you, Ernest Hemingway. Since I forgot to write his name down, as requested, I picked up a lovely copy of *Farewell to Arms*, wonderful book with a bloody awful ending, and I'd love to drop it by. I'll stay only a minute, but it would be my birthday gift.

"May I pick up something on the way? I'd say a coffee, but it's late for that. What about a bottle of wine, or something to eat? All right then. I'll just run the book over, say good night, and hope I can say good bye before I leave tomorrow. Washington, D.C. this time. Another little bookstore there, a library. Must do these things. You did? I hope you enjoyed it. Yes, I suppose enjoy would be the wrong word. Perhaps I should ask if it put you under its spell."

He laughed, thanked her, hung up the phone and leaned back for a kiss from Tina. He sighed as he got up and headed for the bathroom, where he washed his face and looked at his own reflection. He wished he didn't have dark circles under his eyes, but he hadn't slept in over twenty-four hours. The driving, the jitters, and now, one more scene before he could sleep.

He took a lengthy piss, shook his penis thoroughly, and gave it a quick wash with a damp cloth. "Exit, stage left," he said, loud enough for her to hear. "Props: coat, hat, bag of book, and so farewell, my love, until we meet again."

"Break a leg, Brandy."

Lena set the book face down in the white carpet before the red chair and drank the last of her almond-tasting tea, a last goodnight drink. Mystery followed into the foyer, and when she looked back

145

the cat mewed, waving her tail. Lena went to the front door and made certain it was unlocked. "I'm going upstairs," she told the cat.

She took hold of the banister, pulling herself up as she went. She already felt drowsy. Mystery ran ahead and sat in the dark at the top until she arrived, then dashed down the hall to her mother's bedroom door. Lena followed, leaving the door ajar, and Mystery leaped on the bed, crying out.

Lena went to the dresser, looking in the mirror. "I'm sorry," she whispered, "but it was hers. You intended to give it to her." She looked away from the mirror. The cat mewed loudly. "Whatever you have to say, say it." She turned to the mirror. "Why should I be strong? Don't I deserve at least an end to pain?" She set her hands on the dresser and hung her head, her eyes closed.

After a moment's quiet, she went to the bed and lay down on her side, her hands tucked between her thighs. Mystery settled in the crook of her legs, purring.

Rather than knock, Brandon tried the door. When it opened, he stepped in, closed it softly behind him, carrying the bookseller's bag by a string through the top. In the light beside the red chair, he saw his book face down on the floor. He slipped out of his shoes, then his socks, and walked carefully through the living room. The sun porch was dark, leafy and cool.

He looked back through the living room. Nothing stirring. He crept through the living room to the red chair, where he took out the copy of *A Farewell to Arms* he had brought for her and set it on the side table. He shoved the bag in the pocket of his coat and went into the foyer and stood looking up the staircase. He set his foot on the first step, moving quietly, a step at a time, leaning against the wall to listen and to breathe.

He looked down the hallway. The last door on the right was ajar. He tip-toed to it and poked his head inside. He couldn't see anything until his eyes adjusted to the faint light through the curtains. He fancied he could feel the heat from her body, and then he saw light reflected in the eyes of the cat.

"Lena," he whispered. No response.

146

He went to the side of the bed and said, "Lena?"

Still no response. He took the bookseller's bag from his pocket, straightening it. Holding the opening as wide as he could, he thrust it over Lena's head, tightened the string, and held it firmly around her jawline. He did not want to bruise her throat.

When she did not resist, he drew her body to the side of the bed and attempted to pull her to her feet, still no resistance. She crumpled in his arms when he lifted her, cradled against his chest. The cat mewed behind him, but did not leave the bed as he started down the hall with her soft body on his chest. She was lighter even than Tina.

At the top of the stairs, baffled by her apparent willingness to allow him to do as he wished with her, he pulled the bag up, off her face. He could barely see her in the darkness, so he pushed the light switch with his elbow. It might as well have been Tina staring up at him with blank brown eyes. He felt her throbbing life against him. Or, no, was that his own life he felt?

She was unconscious already—this he had not expected. A wave of reluctance passed over him. Was this what all his art and sensitivity came to in the end? Was it too late to call for an ambulance and have done with this insanity? What would Tina say or do if he backed out now, since they had staked their lives on this and nothing else? He leaned on the newel, pulled the bag back over her face and tightened the strings. He faced the stairs and thrust his arms out, setting her aloft. She floated high before thumping heavily half a dozen steps down. She bounced and rolled frantically to the bottom of the stairs.

He closed his eyes and said aloud, "Forgive me," though whether he said this to God or Lena, or even to Tina, he could not be certain. He turned off the light because it made him feel exposed, and then sat on the top step. This was not how he meant to live, not the man he intended to be. He saw nothing before him now, not even the dream of living in this house with Tina. All that lay before him now was retrieving pick and shovel from the trunk of his car and carrying her down to her mother's garden plot.

It was raining lightly, soil wet and heavy in the dark. He heard the trickling of the stream at the back of the yard. Late in the night he worked, lifting shovels full of earth, planting deep a strange new seed in her mother's garden, an act as primal as Cain with his brother. But it was one thing for an ignorant man to perform a violent act and then tremble before his God, but neither of them believed; this allowed them to act as they had, under light of day or dark of night.

Why then did he feel—though hidden by rain and night and trees—that every movement of his arms and shoulders was exposed, as if he stood in an open field, under the sun, performing this uncommon labor? This same feeling came when he revised the engine of the boat: someone was watching him, everything had been discovered, already known. He glanced at the dark upstairs window and felt her watching.

That would be Mystery. She was here, on the dark, wet earth. It pierced him as if she saw herself through his eyes at that moment.

This labor had awaited him from the moment of his birth. All he had to do was go back to his hotel, pick up Lena's sister, and come back to their own house, pretending this had never happened, as if they had no dark stain on their souls. He threw his muddy shoes and tools into the trunk and made a drive he had taken a hundred times in his mind. He needed to cry, but he had no tears, only this dead, dry feeling left inside.

He called Tina from the parking lot of the hotel, while he took his stubby pistol from the glove compartment. When he heard her whispering his name, he set the barrel on his tongue, and noted—as his last sensations—how the taste of metal was so much like blood, how the weight and shape felt in his tightening hand. The darkness swallowed him.

# CHRISTMAS CHARM

WHEN I GOT home from school that day a decade ago, I went to the kitchen, tossed my backpack on the table, and hung on the refrigerator door. I found last night's meatloaf, covered in tinfoil, cut a slice, and sat down to it, no fork needed. I broke off chunks, scarfing it down with a glass of milk. I put the plate and glass in the sink, grabbed my backpack and hurried up the stairs, two or three at a time. "Mom," I called, because I hadn't seen her.

I poked my head in my parents' bedroom and saw her on her back, in jeans and a long-sleeved yellow pullover, mustard yellow, matching the carpet on which she lay. One foot twisted to the side, a slip-on shoe skewered on her big toe, the other on the floor, pointed at the wall. Her dark hair covered her eye and cheek, her mouth slightly open, a red line coming from the corner. I felt rush of hot blood to my head and literally saw red.

I kneeled and repeated, "Mom?" I didn't want to touch her. I held my hand near her face but felt no breath. I held three fingers to her throat, then on her wrist. Mom was a nurse, and she made sure I knew how to respond in an emergency. I could tell right away nothing would bring her back. I saw her cell phone on the floor, at the end of the bed, called 911, and told them what happened, gave the address, and stayed beside her. The police said I seemed self-possessed. They ascertained I had gotten home from school and found her lying there. I went over those moments several times for them, wrote it on a form they gave me. I told them Dad was probably working. He laid concrete driveways, sidewalks, porches, and could be anywhere. I gave them his cell, and when they attempted to call, no one answered because Dad was off murdering the man Mom was seeing, an accountant named Bert Hoskins. She had introduced him to me at a grocery store.

I did not know then what I know now, but I sensed they had history. He wore a light blue shirt, yellow tie, and tan pants, a slender man with gray at the temples and a wide smile. His pale blue eyes took me in longer than necessary. He said he heard good things about me. No man had ever looked at me that same way, especially not my Dad, who always wore gray or maybe camo pants with pockets on the thighs bulging with a tool or two, muddy brown work boots. He had a gray sweatshirt he wore if it was cold. Things like that didn't bother him. He rarely worked in the dead of winter. He hung out with guys who worked for him, making plans, shooting the breeze, a coffee in the morning, beer in the afternoon. He loved his football on weekends, with these guys over. Muscles stood out in his hefty arms.

I don't imagine it took much strength to strangle Mom. She was what they call petite—thin little neck. Now that I think of it, she would have been better matched with the accountant. I worked with Dad in the summers, half a foot shorter and fifty pounds lighter. He used to feel my arms, tell me he was putting muscle on them. He wanted me to take supplements to build weight, but I had to keep it down to 145 for wrestling. If I got heavier, I'd have to wrestle the big boys.

Next time I saw Dad, he was in jail, and then in court. He explained what happened, and like so many, said he just snapped. He'd seen them out, put two and two together, and he lost it. Mom went down in less than a minute. He went looking for Hoskins with a five-shot pistol from the drawer of his nightstand. He gave him two in the face because he hated the way Bert looked at him, three in the chest to finish him off.

I've seen pictures. Mom was a good-looking woman, a case of beauty and the beast. She liked music, Dad tolerated it, with beer. Mom wanted to see the latest movies, Dad thought TV took care of that. She liked to dance, Dad had three left feet. Mom wanted me to go to college, Dad wanted me to work with him when school finished. When I saw her on the bedroom floor, it was like seeing myself dead.

He pleaded guilty and got twenty-five to life. His older sister, Mavis, who looked about like Dad, moved into our house to take care of me, a big laugh. I don't want to go into that fiasco except to say she viewed me as a juvenile delinquent who deserved not much more than a peanut butter sandwich for dinner. It was me and her until I graduated and got away from that house. I avoid thinking of that time. I visit Dad as often as possible, and, to tell the truth, he has a good attitude about it. He seems glad to see me when I come, not in the least embarrassed.

When I went to see him in August, before school started senior year, he told me of some cash he'd hidden in a blue plastic bin at the bottom of a stack of maybe eight of them. If I needed clothes, books, lunch money, I could raid the bin, which I did as soon as I got home. I drove the old Pontiac with a loud muffler. It never went faster than it did that day. I sat on the cold cement counting out two thousand six hundred and forty-eight dollars. First thing I did, I went out for a burger, fries, and a milk shake and wolfed it down.

I drove to Irv's and shot the bull with him a while before we went over to Chick Blank's house, where we bought a baggie filled with red-tinted pot that sent us soaring. We talked about what we wanted from life: getting laid and getting money. I told him that Dad gave me a hundred bucks or so. I had a sense I should keep the whole amount secret. I had it with me, inside pocket of my jacket, but I counted off a hundred in his bathroom so I wouldn't spend more the first day.

We went to a drive-through and picked up a six pack, no questions asked, and sat in the car at the school drinking. It got dark, no one else around, so we broke a window, sneaked in and wrote stuff on the girls' bathroom walls and laughed our heads off. We went around the school. I had butterflies in my stomach, scared I suppose, but had a good time. Irv did too, but he got tired of it, so we left. I took him home and went home myself, where Mavis watched "Law & Order" and drank vodka in the living room. I didn't even tell her good night.

I mentioned she looked like Dad, an exaggeration except for the features, round, thick, without the humor in his face. Just a large

151

bump of some kind beside her nose, and thick glasses. She had his curly hair, longer, more unkempt, and wore what I'd call sack dresses, a faded blue or something. She wore fuzzy slippers in the house, had the paunchy gut, and looked rumpled. She filled the house with cigarette smoke. Mom always made Dad go out back to smoke, but no one told her not to smoke in the house so I did too.

I also smoked dope in my room, opening the windows on even the coldest nights. I hated hanging around the house. About eleven or so, I headed out the back door. Mavis had television up loud because she was half deaf and usually fell asleep in the recliner. She burned holes in the arm and soaked the chair with vodka when she fell asleep with a glass in her hand. I'd hang out in the yard in my jacket and knit cap, on the lawn furniture, drinking beer. That got boring after a while. There was a tall wooden fence around the back yard. A girl from my school lived on the other side, with her younger sister and her parents. It got more interesting when I watched her get ready for bed or whatever, in the bathroom window. She turned on the light and went at her face, putting on some crap for acne. I could only see her from the shoulders up, usually with a bra, but it was nice watching her. Her skin glowed a little. The light shined on her blonde hair.

After a while lights in the house went out. I liked watching that happen, but it made me sad, not just because the show was over. It made me sad to see that house grow dark. I wondered what it would be like to go to bed in that house. One night I went over the fence and looked in all the windows to see what I could see. They left a kitchen window open so I crawled in, sat on the couch, ate something from the fridge. I left the way I'd come. I didn't have nerve to go upstairs, but I hadn't felt so excited about anything since Mavis came.

I didn't go back right away, but I used to think about that experience when I sat in the backyard at night, watching her get ready for bed. When all the lights went off, I'd think of being inside in the dark. I noticed houses either side, started exploring, checking out other houses in the neighborhood. A couple of times, I hid from patrol cars, and that was a little exciting. Next house I tried, I didn't see cars in the driveway. I cut the screen, got a window open and climbed in. This time I went upstairs, checked out bedrooms, searched through drawers. I had no feeling for this house because I didn't know who lived there. When I looked at the photos, they might have been stock pictures stuck in to sell frames. A couple of young kids, their parents, plus an old man with white hair who wore a baseball cap, grandpa, I knew by the look of it.

I tried other houses, but I would scope them out in the daytime so I knew who lived there. I made notes about who lived where, addresses, what kind of dogs, cars, ways to get in. I avoided places with noisy dogs and night with full moons. I wore a sweatshirt now, jacket and cap, but I also wore surgical gloves, from a box of fifty I'd bought. I'd throw them in the trash when I got home. One night I stood in front of a dark Christmas tree, presents bulging beneath, stockings on the mantel, the works. I went through them and selected a small gift to take with me, shoved it in my pocket.

It occurred to me I could take off my clothes and no one would know. I wandered in the kitchen, located alcohol, poured a drink, added ice cubes, gulped it down. I fixed another to take with me upstairs. I didn't make much noise on the stairs. I heard heavy breathing. When I looked in the master bedroom, I saw them on the bed, in the moonlight coming through a window. They didn't know anything about me in the hall, so I leaned in the doorway and watched. I held the ice cubes down with my finger so they didn't make noise. They were also trying not to make noise, because of kids maybe. I walked down the hall to check. Sure enough, one room with bunk beds and a couple of kids asleep, another with a girl a couple of years younger than me.

When I went back to the parent's room, the woman lay with her back to me in moonlight, a nice sight until I heard the toilet flush, the husband in the bathroom. Time had come to get out. I started down the hall as fast as I could when he stepped out buck naked. I rammed into him. He bellowed and grabbed at me so I pushed him. Down he went, head over feet, it looked like, down the stairs. The woman called out, "Bill? Is that you, Bill? Are you all right?"

She stood in the doorway of the bedroom, looking at me, but it was darker in the hall than the bedroom. Her eyes didn't adjust quickly, because the paper said she couldn't see the intruder. I ran downstairs, jumping over the husband, running out in the dark. It had started snowing hard by now, huge flakes coming at me, blurring my vision. It had been snowing like this all day, but it really came at me when I ran. It took a long time to get home and sneak back inside. I still had the glass and the present, so I kept them in my bedroom, as a memento.

The papers called this the Christmas Eve home invasion. I didn't read it and tried not to listen when Mavis went on about it. She did love a tragedy. On my way to school one morning, she tried to shove a paper in my face to show me the picture, but I smacked it away and shouted I didn't want to hear any more about them. "Here's this girl, ninth grade, her father in the hospital with a broken neck," Mavis shouted. I ran out the door into this winter wonderland, a world of white everywhere, breathing in spurts. I felt like the ugliest blot in all that snow.

All that day, I wondered how a man could live with a broken neck. A couple of days later Mavis let me know he hadn't. I avoided her after that, so I wouldn't hear any more. That was the end of my life as a cat burglar. I kept waiting for a knock at the door. I stayed close to home but missed exploring the neighborhood. I took something at every house and had the stuff on top of a chest of drawers, including the glass and the present. I left it wrapped, a stiff little card attached to the red ribbon.

I had hit maybe ten places, so I had a collection, the prize a figurine of a woman with a flag across her lap, maybe Betsy Ross, which I used as show-and-tell for a history talk at school. I calmed down after that. It scared the hell out of me, so I just relived visitations, and the trinkets helped with that. I used to drink out of the glass when I ate dinner. By the end of the school year, I had only a couple hundred of Dad's stash, and when I went to see him I'd wear something new I bought with the money. He told me to see a couple of his old friends, and I went to work with them, doing concrete. A couple of years passed of which I recall nothing. I woke up one day and wondered what the hell had happened to me.

Mom wanted me to go to college, but I'd followed in Dad's footsteps. By this time, I had a fat bank account because the room I rented cost only fifty a month. I did nothing but work and drink with Carl and Pete, who insisted on paying since Dad was in jail. I didn't tell them when I signed up for a couple of classes at Tri-C Community College, partly because I knew they would ask how it was going. I didn't need the pressure. When I got a B in both, I did tell them and took a few more classes, and continued to do all right.

I took classes in the regular semesters and summers until I finished a two-year degree, an Associate of Arts, and got into Cleveland State. I set sights on Civil Engineering, figuring I'd had experience in the general direction, working with Dad, who liked to hear about my classes when I went to see him. He'd been in ten years when I got my four-year degree. This came at a time a civil engineer could get a job, so I went to work with the city and started making decent money.

Of course, this wasn't the only thing happening. I continued working the whole time, to pay for rent and courses, got financial aid, a loan and a scholarship. I met Sylvia, we became a thing, and life got fuller than it had been since I lost Mom, bad times a thing of the past. I didn't want to remember any of that. I buried those years with Mavis when she died of a cancer in the pancreas—that's where it started. The house was gone because she hadn't been able to pay taxes and so on. Dad said, "Easy come, easy go," but I saw it hurt him.

Not only had his sister died, he'd lost the house he paid for over the years when he and Mom lived there, had me, and raised me in that house and yard and neighborhood. All that was gone, but I had moved out as soon as I could. I'd been living in a tiny apartment when I went to CSU, and my last year, Sylvia did too. She was from the neighborhood I grew up in: cute, brown eyed, dark hair she kept short, a straight little body, not real curvy or anything. When I saw her reading, making dinner, or just getting dressed, she looked so perfect that I wanted to cry. I never thought this could happen. She graduated a year later and started teaching elementary school.

One thing I lost when Mom died was holidays. So, our first Christmas together, we went to Syl's house, a week early to decorate the tree. I met her Mom and twin brothers, one of them tall and blonde, the other short and dark, so funny he kept us in stitches. It was strange being in the old neighborhood, but nice too, like life had come home. They all had the same brown eyes, which made me see they were a family. I had this amazing sense of familiarity when I walked in their house. I also felt out of place and didn't know where to put my arms, but her Mom hugged me and had presents under the tree already, some of them for me.

After trimming the tree, we sat in the darkened living room with a glass of wine, enjoying the Christmas lights, when her Mom started telling family stories. She told about the Christmas, over ten years ago, when her husband died. I have heard people say their skin crawled but never felt it until then. She and her husband shared an intimate moment in bed, talking about the kids and their happiness together, but there had been an intruder in the house. Hot blood pounded in my head. I developed a terrible headache and my mouth went dry. I had a metallic taste on my tongue. I got dizzy, like it was snowing in my head. Sylvia's Mom told about a present she put under the tree that the intruder took, a charm Syl wanted—a shiny Eiffel Tower. She dreamed of going to Paris. If she put it on her bracelet, one day she would get there.

I passed out completely, fell back on the couch. When I came to, maybe a minute or so later, everyone was concerned about me. I could barely speak but managed to tell them I was all right. Syl's Mom brought a damp cloth for my forehead. I told them I had been overwhelmed by their kindness. That was true. Their kindness, when I knew I had been responsible for the death of this woman's husband, Sylvia's father. I had heard her speak about him as the most wonderful man she had known before me, and the stories touched me like no other.

Sylvia knew my father killed my mother, and where he lived as a result, but she hadn't said anything more about her father's death than that she had been fourteen. She couldn't go on, even then, her eyes filled with tears. I told her stories about crazy old Mavis, which we laughed at because I put that far behind me, the wound no more scar tissue. Could any man be happier? I worked for the city, had this wonderful girlfriend, and just when her family took me in, I realized I killed the man her mother and Sylvia and her brothers loved more than life. They felt grateful to him—he gave them everything they had, made sure they were taken care of when he died.

I remembered the house now, why it felt familiar. Before I passed out, everything turned red. I experienced this once before, when I found Mom on the floor. But now, right there in the middle, as if the red spread out from it, was the gift that I had taken from their house, and which I still had in the large, black plastic bag in a closet at our apartment. I brought it with me, telling Syl it was the wreckage of my childhood. I never looked at it but couldn't let it go. At the bottom of the bag somewhere was the gift, in red tissue with Santa heads, big white beards and so on, and red ribbon around it. And still attached, the card that said: *To our beloved daughter, from Mom and Dad!* I had felt so eaten up with jealousy when I first saw that, I took it as revenge on the world from which I had been cast out.

I excused myself and went to the bathroom, where I cried so hard my eyes turned red. I kept blowing my nose, trying to do this so quietly no one would hear. I waited in the bathroom long enough that Sylvia came to the door and asked if I was all right. When I came out, she asked me what happened and put her hands on my cheeks. They felt cool because my face was hot. I didn't know what to say and couldn't look at her.

I told her I had to get out in the cool air for a while. I hoped she would understand. I was so overwhelmed by the kindness of her family that I cracked. I almost said *snapped*, like my Dad told me he had when he strangled my mother. I wanted to go out the back door. I told her I might spend the night at our apartment to get a grip on

157

my emotions. I would be back the next day, but I couldn't stay here now. This felt urgent to me, strange to Sylvia, but she let me go out the back. I told her I had not had Christmas like this since Mom died. She made me promise to call when I got home, and in the morning, before I returned.

"You better get back here, or you'll break some hearts."

She assured me they would understand, but only if I came back. I promised and left, and once in the car I had to fight tears. My ears burned hot, my nose ran like crazy, but I knew I had to get home and get the gift out of the bag. I took everything out. It was the size of Sylvia's little fist. I read the card and opened the gift on the floor. There it was, the charm of the Eiffel Tower, with a tiny clasp for her charm bracelet. I had seen her wearing the bracelet. She got comments from other women and explained the charms. When her Mom wrapped it, her husband was alive. I remember feeling so angry, because of the love I saw in that house, that when I ran at Sylvia's father as he stepped from the bathroom, I held my forearms before me like a football block. I hit him with all 145 pounds and knocked him backwards down the stairs.

As I looked at the charm, I knew my brief period of happiness had come to an end. How could I go on with a secret like this? It would come out. If I didn't face up to what I had done so long ago, it would come apart anyway. The secret would kill me or her, or both. I took a shower, got dressed again, and made myself call like I said I would. She sounded relieved. I told her how much I loved her, her Mom, her brothers. I felt I was saying good-bye, and she heard it.

"You're coming back here tomorrow, right?" she said.

I assured her I would as I went out into a light snow, nothing like that night many years ago. Emotions had gotten away with me. She asked me to pick up wine, and the oranges and nuts in shells her Dad always put in the stockings. When I hung up, I knew exactly what I would be losing. We had a bottle of bourbon in the pantry, untouched, so I started on it until I drifted off to sleep. One thing I understood now, any excuse I had ever made for my behavior in those times would hold no longer. The only thing that stopped me from continuing my rampage back then was killing Sylvia's father, and Mavis telling me about it.

Nights are bad for the guilty and ashamed, but morning brings hope. I slept until nine and took another shower. No snow, but cold, crisp air and low white and silver clouds that promised more. Things seemed a little different to me now. I might be accused of gross selfishness if I told Sylvia what I had done and how it happened, just to ease my troubled mind. It seemed to me in the bright December morning that my punishment could be to hold the secret inside me all my life and make it up to her, her mother and her brothers, in every way I could conceive. I would be the best husband ever, the best son-in-law, if I would be allowed to escape the consequences of my acts as a seventeen-year-old kid I barely remembered.

That was when I conceived of what seemed a way to make this happen, to let chips fall where they may. I drove to the drug store and picked up a new box, velvety like a ring box, and blue wrapping papers with white bells ringing on it, as well as a Christmas card large enough to write in, one that said, *For my darling wife!* I put an arrow between the words 'my' and 'darling' and wrote the word 'future'. I went on to the grocery store to pick up fruit and nuts and wine, and when I got back re-boxed and wrapped the charm. The bells on blue paper rang as I wrote: *I saw this at that antiques and nostalgia shop you like. When I heard your Mom's story, I went back, hoping it hadn't been sold. I give you this with hope that over the years, I can be what your father was to you and your Mom and brothers.*

I would watch when she opened it Christmas morning. I would watch her face and those of her mother and brothers to see what would happen next. She called to find out if I had left, and when I would get there, but I did not return her call. Snow had started for real as I listened to her message on the road, windshield wipers slapping, visibility worse by the second. I knew I would not wait for Christmas morning. I would give it up as I came through her door. Other cars pulled off the road, but I plowed ahead, leaning forward

159

in the rush of snow, faster, as if speed could avert the inevitable disaster.

# GREEN'S HISTORY

IT SOMETIMES SEEMS, even to me, a bit strange I've taken such an interest in the age-old question of a perfect crime, though it is true many have given their private hours to lower considerations, how to get the next drink, for example. At any rate, I hardly know how I could have avoided it, just as I couldn't have avoided being who I am, by which I mean myself. I should be more specific at the outset: I mean the perfect murder, in general, and how to commit it, in specific. I have considered the problem from every side, every angle, taken it as it came, by inspiration, and when it did not come naturally, by force, as we take everything to which we have committed ourselves.

The first level is the simplest one, certainly, and avoids, excuse me, I mean involves that nearly mythical presence in our civic and imaginative lives, the police. How to keep from alerting them, how to lull them into sleep, and into remaining asleep, that's the trick, but it's a mug's game—a gangster cliché, I believe, as I hardly know what I mean by a mug—trying to outwit The Men in Blue. In many times and societies, the color of the law enforcement uniform would vary. In Nazi Germany, the greatest fear was of The Man in Black, though, for my contemporaries, that would probably mean Death, or, more familiarly, Mr. Death.

How do I, or to be more speculative, how would I, as a self-consciously educated man, consciously accomplish what a 'mug' might as naturally as breathing: escaping the notice of The Men in Blue in the commission of a heinous crime? We are all familiar with the concept of smelling crime, as if police were cartoon dogs in uniforms alerted to wrong-doing by their noses! Ludicrous. Though, of course, this is exactly how an educated man begins to think, isn't it? Perhaps even why an educated man might turn to crime: to leave the cold world of the ideal and enter a world more immediate, more unconsciously alive. How thrilling to think a phrase like *Murder will out!* But will it, really, must it always? Statistics tell us no, not invariably. Part of the problem is not to set off bells and whistles, not to stir up the scent of crime, to leave a crime scene, if you will, soundless, odorless—to leave it in the intellect, where the police can never find it.

Policemen need a bloody glove, don't they, a dagger wiped clean of prints, a pistol in the trash can, a body in a trash bag in the back-alley dumpster, don't they? That's what police want, isn't it? The scent of the stirrings of the improper in the physical world.

It once seemed the best way to keep the aroma of murder from leaking into the physical world would be to seal it hermetically in the mind, but how does one get a physical deed to remain in the mind, other than by not doing it? I thought I had the answer, back then, but perhaps it was simply that the obsession was greater. I almost sweat to think of it now, but then almost sweating doesn't count, does it, not even in horseshoes. Have you ever heard someone say, You could have killed me! Or, I almost died! Again, ludicrous. No almost in killing or in dying, where anything short of all is nothing.

When killing someone you must complete the act or you have only attempted to kill; true you might do a botch job, only maim and let blood, but then your victim should more truly report, You stabbed me. I knew a young woman once caught briefly under the boat on a white-water rafting trip who said repeatedly that she almost died. It seemed to be a delight to her the longer she repeated it, even though there is no condition such as almost dead. "I walked around for several weeks almost dead" should read "half-dead." If you didn't die were you ever almost dead? If you were truly almost dead, you would eventually become dead; once you died you could not use that "almost dead" business. Would you almost call the doctor to very nearly have your symptoms checked? Do you see what I mean?

I begrudgingly admit there might be sense to walking around muttering under your breath that you very nearly killed someone or other, but, generally, such a statement is a gross exaggeration and cannot be said with any reasonable expectation of being taken for the truth. When people tell you they almost died, they almost always—all these wretched qualifiers—mean they avoided death altogether, yet here he or she stands, whole as Harry Houdini, when she or he might have been otherwise, to wit, not living.

Almost dying, almost killing, a bit like the teenage girl who told her parents she might be a little pregnant, or in the case of the young man, I got her a little pregnant. She is or is not pregnant; he is or is not a Daddy—though, I suppose, in the case of abortion there might be some leeway for such speech. I only wish I did not have to be so fair about everything myself. A more stupid and effective man might simply make his case and hold his tongue without dreaming up loopholes for the other guy. The question could be more clearly stated: Can a crime like murder—no, let us say, can a murder be contained within the mind of the murderer to the extent that no foul scent whatsoever leaks, or, further, that there is in fact no foul odor, no stink, to be blunt, yet still be an actual murder occurring in historical reality?

Well, that is what interested me for a great while, even at work, walking through the hallways at school, passing through so many humid adolescent bodies bumping about like clumsy moths, absorbed perhaps defensively in my own thoughts, locking them away from everyone around me, everyone I passed, my amused eyes glazed or distracted, as people sometimes said: He's in his own world! "Thinking of something else." No one penetrated my inner sanctum, that was the idea: How to keep from being diminished in the handling of so many hands, so many fingers, so many indifferent fingerprints.

That's what summers are for, those winter breaks and weekends! Don't we have a right to our own lives? Is this privacy we so lovingly discuss more than an abstraction? Or have most of us, in truth, given over our private lives, private minds, privacy itself, to the collective, one way or another? To co-workers, neighbors, clerks and congressmen, to the president and homeland security? To any nincompoop we met on the street! Don't we give them all molecules of ourselves so easily that keeping anything secure in our private minds would first entail owning one's own privacy. I can't speak for everyone, but in a democracy, I should only have to speak of my own private mind. Wouldn't the first step of actually owning a private mind be to keep others out, without becoming defensive, paranoid, with a glad heart and a positive spirit, so that my own privacy would be worth keeping?

I determined some years ago that I would find a way to seal my mind, or a significant piece of my mind—you have heard people say, I gave him a piece of my mind, so speaking of the mind in pieces is not entirely unfamiliar (render unto Seizer what is Seizers)—off from the world pleasantly, so my pleasantness, my unobjectionable nature would be one of the very tightest seals with which I locked a piece of my own mind, which I would call my mind proper, off from the world.

I practiced my smiling in a mirror until I found the perfect, most defeating smiles of all, my most usable smiles, smiles that would least pain my face, that would not create more problems than they solved—inappropriate laughter or smiling is one of the most universal signals of madness—and then practiced those smiles in public situations for the responses they elicited. Having chosen a group of four or five smiles, two or three of them most effective, I began employing them in shutting the doors of my private mind until that part of me ceased to exist in the collective.

I established a routine for grooming and medical care so regular I marked them on the calendar throughout the year. To start with, a haircut, a trim really, every two weeks, varying barber shops so they would become interchangeable, so I would never have to concern myself with the leaving of a favorite stylist or the closing of my favorite shop. I refused to be picky about which doctor or dentist saw me, choosing a practice on the basis of the number of doctors involved, so I would never have to change offices on the death or retirement of one person. I visited my dentist every six months, doctor likewise; no unattended ailments would put me at the mercy of my fellow man. My vision, always perfect, I have checked once a year. I trust doctors and barbers implicitly and leave my care in their hands. I smile at everyone. Slow or impossible to anger, even on the road. The world rolled off my back like water off a buck's dack, to vary the cliché.

My apartment was pleasant, my plants attended by a service. My bird, a blue parakeet named Budgie, pleasant and interchangeable. My dinners at home and out, all pleasant and interchangeable. Lesson plans for school took a minimum of mind, as did regular and persistent study in my field. A newspaper every day, with one of my meals, committing useless facts to memory for as long as necessary. How do the Browns look this season? Well, I hope the new quarterback works out. The last one had flat feet. I began to take ownership of my own mind.

And I put something in my private mind so I would know it always, and it would know me and no one else would know. I put inside my mind a thought that no one else would know, no one, and by this I attained pure privacy. The drama my own, the stage my mind. By this I knew myself to be myself, separate from all smiles and pleasantness by which the world knew me: one day I would kill someone and get away with it.

This morning as I stood in front of the full-length mirror on my bedroom wall to brush my hair—a mirror I am so used to using I forget it is there, even when I am using it—I noticed a man looking out of the mirror, directly into my eyes. He had so much reality I had the distinct sense he wondered why I should be the one to walk out into the world while he remained in the mirror. It occurred to me that he had a life in the mirror attached and connected to my acts and gestures in a way I could never understand. I felt he resented either my primacy, or, at the very least, my presumption of primacy.

I do not imagine I am the first person who has ever had such thoughts, but I felt them with such force and he studied me with such intensity that I became afraid. I do not think of myself as a frightened man, but my eyes watered. He might have been thinking the perfect crime would be to murder me and retreat to his side of the mirror forever, never to return. It made sense, I realized, that those thoughts I ascribed to him he might also ascribe to me. As I

165

turned to leave, heading off to school, I could easily imagine with what thoughts he walked away from me, never looking back.

I wrote that I woke last night, 3:21 by the large red numerals on my alarm clock, aware of two things: that backwards the numerals read 1-2-3, and that I could not go back to sleep. I turned on the lamp, sat on the edge of my bed, set my notebook on my knees and wrote the incident which immediately precedes this one. When I completed the entry, I had the thought that I had never really hurt anyone in a great number of years. For some this might be a comforting thought, but for me, just a thought.

I set the notebook on my bedside table, turned out the light, swung my legs onto the bed, and drew the covers. I woke again, as usual, just before the alarm bells chimed at 5:30, got up, showered, shaved, had a morning movement, brushed my hair in the mirror without incident, fixed an egg and toast with first orange juice and then coffee. I ate in white undershirt and undershorts, then washed the dishes.

I put on a pale green oxford shirt, a pair of gray pants, slipped on black socks and black penny loafers, and sat once more on the edge of my bed, taking a moment to write before I left for school. I took a moment to look over my notes on the brief presidency of James A. Garfield, who was from Cleveland, amazed that I had to give an entire day to his term, but I had, over the years, garnered many vignettes of his personal and political life, none any more engaging than the story of his assassination.

Most scenes of assassination, set side by side in photographs and in artist's renditions, are cut from the one cloth; assassins vary as to range of madness and purpose. Charles Guiteau became a victim of outrage when his application for American Ambassador to France had been passed over by Garfield's administration, and so he set about proving the soundness of their decision by attempting to kill the President. God told him that he must shoot the president, shoring up his instinct to do so without prodding. I provide no commentary on the frequency with which God seems to whisper barbarities to men possessed by outrage or loneliness or love. In one series of murders, He spoke through a neighbor's black Labrador Retriever.

The story is well known except to high school students, so I get to tell it to them for the first time. Garfield was not actually killed by Charles Guiteau, who ambushed him on a train to visit his sick wife in Elberon, New Jersey. Garfield was not a victim of assassination at all. Guiteau hired a hansom to take him to a prison in Washington he had already scouted, but police dragged him off in one direction and poor Garfield in another, toward their respective ignoble fates. For Garfield, that meant death at the hands of doctors who probed his wounds with unsanitary fingers that most likely led to the infection which caused his heart attack. They could not find the bullet lodged only three inches in his flesh and called in a Great American Inventor, Alexander Graham Bell, and his metal detector, a new technology with which he gauged the bullet pierced more deeply than doctors originally imagined. Unfortunately, his detector had located a bed spring immediately beneath the body of the President of the United States, which caused the good doctors to probe yet another twenty inches into Cleveland's Favorite Son.

I tell students unless we learn history, we are doomed to repeat it. I tell them they should not let this incident color their sense of the reliability of our political or medical institutions. I tell them Garfield was a great American, a great Clevelander. By the time they leave they barely remember that one of our duly elected presidents was killed by his doctors. He was, however, not the first, an honor that resides with George Washington, a man of sixty years, six feet in height, by all accounts robust, who might have recovered from pneumonia, it is speculated, had his doctors not insisted on bleeding him to death.

A most imperfect murder that was: sloppy, messy, openly idiotic. My own preoccupation returns, as always, but only after students leave. Sometimes I am aware of the small lighted private portion of my mind sealed away from public scrutiny in which some previously established drama of quietly ignited murder is progressing as if I dreamt in my waking life. It is this by which I know I exist as a private individual, as I have, I believe, already mentioned.

Can anything be more beautiful than a day in autumn which begins with drizzle and the blurring and blending of the colors of leaves, the reds and yellows and browns clinging their last to boughs of wet black trees? Only a day such as I have described on which sunlight suddenly breaks forth to discover the glistening brightness, the grass still green and sparkling even as droplets drip across my window one moment to the next, and a sweet, almost translucent rainbow arches over all!

Lunch in my classroom today, at my desk at the back of a room before which, in six ranks, thirty-six sturdy desks have been arranged before a wooden rostrum and the wide green board I love so much, on which still parades names and dates and places that make up our sense of history, pillars and posts of a national identity I am charged with passing on to the youngest generation of Americans. I like to think I do it well, responsible both to truth and to our fondest hopes and dreams.

I do not take my job lightly; my students rarely misbehave, and quite a few take notes. I encourage them to be good citizens, to register and vote when their hour comes. A few have come back to tell me what I meant to them. To a few I mean nothing at all. I am pleasant, rigorous, fair. Of that other obsession, not one knows a thing. This began six years ago—only six years! But set itself up with such force it seems I have known it all my life. Perhaps I should tell you the first clumsy moment I became what I am today. I had driven downtown to return a few books to the library and walked across the street for a pound of coffee beans from Raymond's. I had brought my gas bill and walked across the open, concrete mall where the city often provides concerts of the local orchestra or bands at lunchtime or on weekends, well attended I might add, to the gas company building on the other side.

Our municipal government is sound. Downtown has not been forgotten. No child has been left behind. Snow clearing is good in winter so it is rare to flounder on my way to or from school. Our Mayor has a prominent place in the State and nationally, among City Mayors. It is my contention we can be proud of our elected leaders, and in my memory, I recall only one Mayor who ought to have been tarred and feathered; fortunately for us, unfortunately for Ohio, he went on to become a State Senator, elected on a simple alliterative name easily remembered in the voting booth.

I carried with me a newspaper and a coffee in a paper cup, and, of course, the gas bill; I enjoy paying bills in person. I took a moment to sit down on a free bench and spread the paper across my lap, the coffee beans in my lap beneath the paper, my coffee perched on the armrest. City employees, employees of various lawyers and banks in the area sat about eating lunches at tables, on benches, at the edge of the fountain, talking earnestly, enjoying the sun and the air before they must return to their labors.

For me, it had been a morning of meetings preliminary to the start of a new year; I would return for more afternoon meetings. This moment felt as pleasant to me as to anyone gathered in the mild noonday sun. I read in the paper an editorial relating to a law passed by the State that allowed carrying a concealed weapon by anyone who applied for and was granted a permit. Gun toting Americans reliving a Cowboy past. It actually inspired me. What would it be like sitting in the open air of the mall with a loaded weapon in my pocket, under my armpit, in a holster at the small of my back, hidden by a jacket? Would I actually be safer, as proponents suggested; was I presently in danger?

And what if I had a loaded pistol on my person? I could walk to the back of one of these benches, behind someone at a table, and blow their brains out. The thought thrilled me, but I did not yet know what it meant or why. How could I shoot one of our unsuspecting citizens and go undetected by others? A small pistol, nearly invisible in the palm of the hand, perhaps a .44 caliber Derringer like the one Mr. Booth used to shoot President Lincoln to avenge Lee's surrender at Appomattox. April, 1865. Good Friday. Believing himself an instrument of God.

It would be better to have an unregistered weapon. I leave to pay my bill at the other side of the mall, kapow, the quiet little pistol barks behind the beans and newspaper in my left mitt, then on to the gas company! Behind me, a dumpy citizen slumps, falls to the concrete as I enter the building and step to a window behind one or two debtors, one of whom furrows her thick brow as she sees a commotion outside the window.

"What is that?" she says, without looking at me.

"Hmmn?"

"Somebody must have had a stroke. Or a heart attack."

"Really?"

"Next," calls the anorexic red-haired man behind the window, and the thick browed lady forgets everything but the check she needs to write.

I don't even look behind me.

Zwoop, back in the bench. I bump my cup off the armrest, the lid pops, coffee spills all over the white concrete. I walk toward the Gas Company, beans and newspaper under my arm, humming a tune even I don't recognize.


Single man at the breakfast bar of his favorite franchise orders blueberry pancakes, eggs, bacon, 8:00 of an evening after a busy day at the relative beginning of a new academic year, tells the friendly pregnant waitress this very day in history the twentieth president of the United States, after being shot by an angry office seeker, died of a massive heart attack. Did she know who that was?

"I'm afraid not."

"Think. Cleveland Native."

"I'm sorry, I just don't know," she says, the tip of her pen still touching her pad. "What would you like to drink with that?"

"I will tell you what I would like to drink if you can tell me who he was. And I will throw in an extra five-dollar tip!" Her eyes glaze over. I have seen this in students. I shrug. "Just the water and a cup of coffee, cream."

She makes a notation, starts to walk off, then turns and gives the right half of her smile. "Who was it?" Ah, an interest historical raises its hoary head.

"Garfield."

"Garfield?"

"Exactly."

"I thought he was a cartoon cat."

I smile back at her. "Not always. And not in 1881."

She looks a moment, then turns to hang the order slip on the metal wheel in the long, narrow window. The cook on the other side, a powerful looking black man in a white blouse and a cook's hat, moves steadily, surely, clanging his heavy spatula on the grill to clean it off and create a working rhythm. He is one of the reasons I like to eat here, besides the fact that I have never once gotten sick on the food. When he turns to the order, he lowers his head to see through the window. "Howdy, Professor." Beads of sweat on his forehead. "How's school this year?"

"Very well, thank you, Shawn." I smile wanly, ask if he knows which president, believed the victim of assassination, died of a massive heart attack this day in history.

"I sure do." He winks at me. I laugh out loud, and Shawn turns to his grill. He says it loudly over his back, "Cleveland Native James A. Garfield."

"That's right! An A for you today."

"I could use it." Clang.

I open my notebook and begin to write.

I want to clarify something about this business of thinking about murder: I don't mean this to be a purely intellectual exercise. So much in my life involves the intellectual. I have to keep fresh in my subject by reviewing the latest historical research, favoring the genre I call Gossip about the Dead. With some of these Dead I am especially conversant. A new detail, a good story, some reversal in the common knowledge of an historical event can crack through layers of indifference. Not known as a popular teacher, I try to interest students with ideas, facts, substance rather than manner. The American flag on my lapel, and, just beneath it, the silver cross, announce my politics, but I never use the rostrum as pulpit, except for political and intellectual involvement in the history and future of our nation. Shawn knows this. I never let down because I am truly what I appear to be, and that I consider a primary virtue in a teacher.

My consideration of murder is a relief to normal intellectual activities, something like whittling. Imagining how it might be done, someone could argue, has an intellectual component, but what does not? Though I use my eyes in my profession, I can think of no leisure activity that would allow me to close them except sleeping, of which, however, I am not particularly fond. As I sit in the back of my classroom giving an exam, I do not fantasize about killing one of my students with a desk chair. I pick out someone I have passed during the week and imagine how I might have killed that one without rousing suspicion, artfully, without compunction or regret. I don't actually think it, I see it, just as one might dream, but in a wakeful state, a drama illuminated in the cell of my private mind: an old woman walking down the road carrying a satchel one deserted evening, and not another traveler on the road. A baseball bat out the window as I drive by, not even looking at her, then home, a good bath for the bat, lean it in the basement storage area beside my old baseball glove.

I have no desire to see a poor old woman dead! Or to bludgeon her with a bat! I am interested in how this might have been accomplished without detection. Other images have been more complex, to be sure, but I mention this because the initial incident came and went in a moment, and later, in tranquility, I recalled it with the details of her death worked out by the powers of the waking dream. We might as well get over any revulsion you might have of these little dramas, so I provide a heinous example. Hate me quick and get over it.

Did I kill her? No, I swerved to give her room that she would not feel crowded, then gave a wave and a practiced genuine smile. It was only later I killed her. History teaches us events that do not happen are of no consequence. A game, to assure me that I have a private life and to exercise some small degree of control over my natural fear of death: or so I theorize. As it does not enter my daily activities, I judge it healthful, contributing to my general sense of wellbeing. Sublimating natural predatory instincts. Redirecting a murderous impulse into a harmless outlet. Jigsaw puzzle, brain teaser. involving my sense of art, of dance, of drama, ritual and romance.

One reason I enjoy seeing Shawn so much, not just as a former student and lively grill cook, is because I have a fully formed dream of how I might kill him as he leaves the restaurant after closing, as I once observed him passing late one night after watching a student play in the auditorium, and stopping by—at the players' request—the cast party, having performed small tasks of research concerning costumes and props. I stood among them sipping a coke, laughing at happy, victorious jokes for over an hour before I slipped out and drove home, stopping at O'Malley's for a bottle of beer—I'd rather have a bottle in front of me than a frontal lobotomy, said Dorothy Parker—before driving past my favorite franchise to see if pancakes and eggs might be had at this late hour.

That was when I saw Shawn tossing bags of garbage into the fetid dumpster as I pulled behind the building. I sat there a moment as Shawn raised one arm over his eyes, blinking into my headlights. I saw it all immediately, in a flash of inspiration which I will not go into out of respect for my former student, except to say one word: glorious.

When I watch Shawn's elegant, powerful back as he moves over the grill, and consider his history in my class—a gallant lad, a decent scholar, kind at heart—and recall that moment of illumination at the dumpster, my heart is happier and fuller. He becomes a work of casual and unerring art, submitting to his death and disposal as naturally as he took in a pass downfield at twenty yards. I am committed to one day being there for him, to help his kids succeed in school, make their way in college. I listen closely to conversations he has with the other cook, a hefty woman with yellow hair tied back in a pony tail tucked in a hair net under her white hat. Or with the pregnant waitress, who admires him as we all did and do to this day. I want one hint of what I might do for him, if anything can be done.

I have none of these generous feelings for principle, vice principle, school superintendent, each of whom I have killed in undetectable ways that gave me the power I need to go on with a life, as Henry David Thoreau (a great admirer of the violent activist John Brown, whose body lies moldering in the grave) has said it, "of quiet desperation." Could Thoreau imagine such escape as I have achieved?

Ah, pancakes arriving. I stop to give grateful attention to Margie, whose eyes are directed slantwise at the fellow two seats down talking loudly on his cell phone. P.S. As she set the plate before me, she leaned and whispered, "Now there's someone I'd like to shoot." I smiled, nodded, smelled deeply the aroma of blueberries.

"That," I whispered back, "would be justifiable homicide."

She winked at me. "Enjoy your hotcakes, Mr. Green."

"Good morning, Future Voters of America!"

That's how I begin classes, though I vary it. Of course, students see playful irony, but I like to think they also see that I am serious about the necessity of understanding history as it is. It is not my job to pretty it up or make it more horrible than it was: history is as horrible as it ought to be. Most of them were five or six when Timothy McVeigh blew up the Alfred P. Murrah Federal Building in 1995, killing somewhere in the unfriendly neighborhood of three hundred Oklahomans, claiming to avenge the deaths at Ruby Ridge and Waco inflicted by Federal Law Enforcement officials, a boy who liked bombs better than ballots. As they graduated from junior high O.B.L. blew up The Twin Towers to prove another point. High school students shot up classmates and presidents attacked foreign powers while they played Barbies and Baseball, getting that first kiss, taking their driving tests while nut-sacks with bombs strapped to their torsos splashed gore on shop walls of pizzerias. Killers who ate their prey played across the big screen. Violence is nothing new to them, but the nature and the uses of violence, *that* history clarifies. What happens in their lifetime does not happen for the first time in the world.

"World War I," I said, "happened a long time ago. Anyone tell me when? Pete. No, I 'm sorry, that was the Civil War. How much after the Civil War did WWI occur? Longer than that. Closer. Who in your family was alive in World War I? That's right. Your great grandfathers and grandmothers witnessed the bloodiest, deadliest, most horrifying war in history and survived it or most of you would not be in this room. Many did not. Their children's children are not in this room.

What started it all, Ladies and Gentlemen? No, sorry Natalie, the Nazis didn't come to power for another twenty years. Your grandparents had to fight them in the bloodiest, deadliest, most horrifying war in history, a war that established the United States as the first economic power in the world, since the nations who hosted the war had been decimated by it. Yes, Cory, Saving Private Ryan told the story of one of the pivotal battles on the European front, but we are speaking now of World War I and what started it. Anyone?"

My method is not exactly Socratic, but I don't let them remain uninvolved.

Guess what started it: assassination. Of whom? I'm afraid that's many years later, Pete, in 1963, Dallas, Texas. No more guessing. I am now certain none of you know the answer. In those days, power was arranged differently. Austria-Hungary was an empire, a major world power, and Archduke Franz Ferdinand, let me spell that on the board, was an Austrian Royal, governor of the provinces of Bosnia-Herzegovina, a violent region even in our own time, if I can just get this old map down without tearing it: Sarajevo. Winter Olympics held here some years ago, before it was destroyed by ethnic conflict. Many Bosnians, especially a population called Serbs, were unhappy their lands were governed by outsiders. One of the eternal rules of governance: no one likes outsiders telling them what to do. What do they want to do to these outsiders, generally speaking? That's right, Pete, A for the day: they want to kill them. But why are we talking about events half a world away? What difference do distant affairs make in our lives? That's right, folks, Carrie's older brother is serving his country in Iraq right now.

Your mother, James? I take my hat off to her, I salute them all. They don't ask what difference events in distant lands make. They know the basic organizing principle of the world is violence; how much stronger one well-placed bullet than a well-considered vote. The world found out when Gavrilo Princep pulled a trigger on Franz Ferdinand and all those boys on farms in Nebraska signed up for war to save Paris from a German takeover. Their acts changed not only history but our country forever. And, so did the act of one angry, proud man who didn't want foreigners telling his people what to do.

Does anyone know what differentiates the act of Timothy McVeigh from the act of Gavrilo Princep? Take this down in your notebooks or listen. Timothy did absolutely nothing to change the world. His was a fruitless act that brought only heartbreak. What was changed? Only this: we know that not every terrorist is a foreigner. Is this what Tim died to achieve? He had no more affect than those knuckleheads at Columbine who shot up their school. They might have achieved more by setting themselves aflame after mailing to principle, teachers, newspapers a list of grievances. Instead, they are whiners, fools and cruel heads. Squeaky Fromm, a Charley Manson lunatic, was stopped from even pulling the trigger on the bland President Gerald Ford who had done nothing but step into the White House briefly after Nixon left office and would do little before being beaten in the next election by Jimmy Carter.

What did Squeaky have to gain? She squeaked as they hauled her off.

Pathetic John Hinckley III shot Ronald Reagan, the movie star president, sent him to the hospital, and severely wounded James Brady, why? If we are to believe the story, because he wanted to impress a movie star! Now he gets to visit with his parents as long as they keep him on a leash: idiots, wastrels! Sirhan Bishara Sirhan, who shot Bobby Kennedy because of his support for Israel, a reason no one understood at the time, did his time in solitary at Soledad where an inmate gouged out an eye with a spoon, also gaining what we call nothing at all.

Gavrilo? The day before, their plot had broken down when a bomb thrown at the Archduke's open car exploded without killing anyone but spectators that kept the assassins from getting closer. Next day, June 18, 1914, Ferdinand and his wife went to visit the wounded. His driver made a wrong turn, and, trying to get out of the street, backed slowly past an impromptu Gavrilo who switched from buying a sandwich on Franz Joseph Street to drawing a Browning semi-automatic pistol and stepping into the path of history, firing from a distance of four or five feet, as far as from me to Pete, into the belly of Ferdinand's pregnant wife Sophia—the Archduke cried out for her to wake up—then into the Archduke himself.

Gavrilo tried to swallow cyanide—an assassin should always die in the attempt—but vomited, attempted to shoot himself, was arrested and sentenced to twenty years in prison, where he died four years later at the age of, attention please, twenty-three, of Tuberculosis of the bone. How old was Gavrilo Princep when he shot the Archduke, James? That's right. Nineteen. And how old are you? Just two years younger than Gavrilo who changed the course of history: a world at war for his act. Nineteen years old, unafraid to get involved in the fate of his nation. The Browning he used is on display at a museum in Vienna, the bullet in a castle in the Czech Republic.

For this your grandfathers were called from farmlands and shops! For this your grandparents delayed families and lives. A new world was born out of the fire that would come again just two decades later to finish the job. Gavrilo Princep, nineteen, wrote his name in history books, and his cry, as he fired, might have been the same as the notorious John Wilkes Booth leaping from the box at Ford's Theater: *Sic Semper Tyrannis!*

177

# THE LOST BOY

WHEN NEWS THAT a child had disappeared rippled through the neighborhood, we answered the call. I'd been living here eight years and hadn't had many conversations with neighbors on my street. For one thing, everyone on Shaggy Birch Loop was Catholic except me and the older couple next door who didn't talk with anyone. Their son had died at some point in the past, over eight years ago, and they had become withdrawn. The only time the man spoke to me was to ask if he could cut down a sturdy poplar on our property line, for firewood. He was a man my size in a red flannel shirt, wrinkled brown slacks, and work boots. He sometimes wore glasses with clear frames. He had thin brown and gray hair. By the time I got home from work, all that remained was a stump, the logs stacked neatly on top of his woodpile, the prettiest white wood with a dark core at the center. I had to run my hand over the smooth top of the stump.

The son had been a young man of nineteen or twenty, and drugs had been involved. I don't know if they had any religion, but I know they didn't go to St. Martha's. Perhaps they once had. I went quite a few times myself and tried to join. My first wife and I divorced, so I would have to file a petition to have the marriage annulled retroactively. This involved a questionnaire with some ninety questions, and I would have had to ask a couple of friends or family members to fill out another such questionnaire, to establish the flaw that invalidated our marriage, as if it had never been. I would also have to pay a five-hundred-dollar legal fee for a cannon lawyer to declare my previous marriage invalid and then remarry Catherine in the church, otherwise we would not be considered married at all. They might have thought that Laura's claiming to be an atheist was enough of a flaw to begin with. We did have arguments, like any couple, but I didn't want the marriage declared invalid, so I gave up and quit going.

I didn't regret anything except the break-up, which came after seven years. Laura had a chance to work overseas, in Sweden, but I did not want to just leave my job here and my family. I wasn't likely to find something better than the university, where I was an I.T. guy. My parents and brother and sister lived within an hour's drive. Laura and I tried the long-distance marriage a while, but that ended when she met a German man and fell in love. I'm happy for her, I told her so. She wanted me to meet Wolfgang. I'd like to, I told her, but I had no interest in meeting him. And then when Catherine and I married, it was out of the question. Catherine and I work together at the university, same department. She had a brain tumor when she was fifteen that left her blind in one eye and with no a sense of smell.

But about my first marriage, the story was simple: I loved her and she loved me. Now she had a child, son of a German man, whose name was Hans. Laura and Wolfgang, and little Hans, who has her blonde hair and rosy cheeks. That was behind us now, but I did not want that seven years of my life declared invalid, which must mean that I am not meant to be a Catholic. I go on as I am, as nothing, same as Catherine, square pegs in a neighborhood of round holes, along with the neighbors whose son died. The only thing that connects me to this neighborhood is coaching soccer at the junior high team. They pay me a modest sum, but that's not why I do it. I played in high school and in college and wanted to keep it going. This was early in November. Our season had ended on the weekend, when we lost a semi-final game we should have won, 1-4.

When I heard a kid had gone missing, I followed people moving in that direction until I got to a house with a cruiser out front, low blue and red lights swirling. It turned out the kid was actually thirteen-year-old Peter Johns. He had been one of my players this season. I reprimanded him at our last game, which felt lousy now. A policeman hooked me up with a couple of men I'd never met, all of us carrying different flashlights. It was getting dark as groups split up in various directions. We had the upper streets of the neighborhood to search.

The development went up in the late sixties, a couple hundred houses, probably more. I hadn't ever counted. Developers purchased this land from farmers who had worked these fields for a few generations. On the upper side, Cardinal Road separated the houses and people from a wooded area that had been there longer than that. Wooded parcels would be developed one day soon, we had been told, with houses more expensive than ours on smaller lots. Ours had no lots smaller than half an acre, most of them a little bigger. The rule had been instituted that no fences could be erected around any lots, to keep the open flow of the land. All of us had septic tanks and wells, but there had been some discussion whether to hook up to city water. I had no opinion on the matter. I liked picking up an enormous bottle of drinking water each week from Clearwater, on my way home. I'd turn it upside down on the cooling stand I got from them. Most neighbors had it delivered, but I liked to go personally. City dwellers called this living out in the country. Catherine and I lived out in the country, in the same house Laura and I did.

Below the development, the neighborhood trailed into overgrown fields until you got to Moxley Road, where a new development was already going in. A large parcel of land in between had been deeded to the university where I worked, as wetlands preserve, so at least that wouldn't be developed. Our group went through each street of the upper neighborhood, knocking on doors to make sure Peter hadn't disappeared into someone's house, where he was safely playing video games. We went up to Cardinal while others combed down to Moxley, including university land that had not yet been fenced off. We talked about what might have happened, where he might be, without acknowledging our fear that he had been abducted and taken out of the area altogether.

At eleven thirty or so, the other men in my group called it a night. We exchanged phone numbers, in case we were needed or some news came in. I stayed because I had coached this kid. He was no great shakes as a soccer player, but my philosophy was, if you want to be on the team, I'll get you in now and again. The school did expect me to win some games. My boys fed into a high school team that had always been competitive. I had on boots and jacket, gloves and cap, though it hadn't gotten below forty-five during the day. Temperatures had been falling and might drop into low thirties, high twenties before the night was over. I didn't like to think of Peter out there without proper dress. I felt certain he wouldn't have thought ahead. We split up at the edge of the wooded area across Cardinal, but I still wanted to take a look in there, just in case.

The moon was an edge off full, but it gave light. When clouds drifted across the face, it got darker, and then it would come back. As I moved into the trees, I couldn't have seen much if I didn't have the flashlight, a yellow box affair with one big battery inside. It gave good light and the beam spread. I said his name a few times, but the twigs, branches, and fallen leaves all made enough noise underfoot or as I brushed by that he might not have heard me, if he was anywhere nearby. A fox stood illuminated for a moment, eyes glowing, before it dashed off. One day, coming home from work, I saw a box turtle crossing the road in front of me from these woods. I pulled over and carried it across so it wouldn't get hit by a car. On the other side was a little stream filled with watercress at that time, and then the houses began. I thought maybe he wanted to get at the watercress.

I'd only been in there fifteen, maybe twenty minutes, when I tripped over a big rock. I caught myself with one hand against a tree and stood like that a while, listening to the silence. I heard a few leaves that hadn't yet fallen rattling softly. Dark of night surrounded me, darker than in the neighborhood. I sat on the rock a moment and took cigarettes from my jacket pocket. I had quit at the start of the season, but I hadn't worn this jacket since last year. I had slipped a book of matches under the cellophane, so I lit up and had a smoke. I turned off the flashlight and set it at my feet. It got dark awfully quick. I couldn't see a thing when I turned it off, but my eyes started getting used to the dark, and I could make out the ground and the trees and such. It reminded me of when Laura and I went camping, sitting in the dark by the light of a small fire.

She and Wolfgang lived in Stockholm, as far away as another planet, with this son I'd seen in the photo. It could be snowing there now, six o'clock in the morning. They could still be in bed, or getting up. Laura liked to get up early and fix a pot of coffee. She wrote in her journal with her first cup of the day, so I just ignored her when I got a cup to get ready for work. When I asked what was in it, she told me she wrote about the day before, what she was going to do in the day to come. Sometimes, she wrote down a dream, if it stuck in her mind. She said I could read it if I liked, but I never did. I liked to see her writing at the round dining room table before I took a shower, the privacy of it.

I missed that for the longest time once she left. I expected to see her and she wasn't there. I had to fix the coffee. That made me feel alone. I had been considering getting a dog for quite a while, just to have a creature stirring up the air. My next-door neighbors, on the other side of the older couple whose son died, had a wire-haired fox terrier. When I asked what it was, they used that whole set-up, as if the kind of hair it had was part of its name. White, with black spots. An energetic dog with a sharp, clearly defined bark. Each bark stood out on its own, not like some small dogs where they all run together in a rush. I had seen Joe throwing a stick for Junior. When he had it in his hand, cocked back to throw, Junior came off the ground like he was on springs, as high as Joe's shoulder, five or six times, until he threw the stick, then, off like a shot.

I watched the dog for them one week and let it in the house, just to see what it would be like. But Joe's dog acted like a stranger, sniffing around the whole time. It was weird having the dog in my house, and it made me wonder why Laura and I never had one, or even a cat. If we'd had a dog, it would have been harder for her to leave, but she would have left the dog there too, I knew that much. So, I was glad we didn't have one. I didn't want it to be any harder on her than it had to be, and the dog would have been lonely for her, which would have depressed me. As it was, I continued to get dressed and go to work, and on some evenings or weekends I coached the boys, but I felt empty space around me, a buffer of silence between me and the rest of the world.

Catherine and I actually do have a dog, one we adopted at a refuge, I guess you'd call it, but she's not all that active. Catherine found her, a solid dog about forty pounds, reddish brown, and completely blind, with her eyes sewn shut so she doesn't scare kids. After Catherine saw her, she cried all night. The next day we went to get her, and she named her Periwinkle. She's a nice dog, and likes to go on walks though she can't see a thing. Catherine says she sees with her nose, which is more than Catherine, who has no sense of smell. She's not completely blind in the bad eye. Catherine sees colors and movement in that one, and there's been talk the damage may be repairable, so she could get some back. She repeated tenth grade because of this tumor, laid up with surgeries. That's when she learned about computers, stuck at home. She's a quiet woman, a good companion who goes along with anything I want and usually seems happy about it. She has a sweet smile, short red hair, and pale green eyes. Sometimes I get disturbed when she sits on the couch staring out the window vacantly, the bad eye nearest me. It scares me until she turns to me and gives me the smile, and it's all right. She's a hard worker, very dependable, and we end up going out for dinner quite a bit, because we come home tired.

It was dark and cool in the trees, and I smelled dirt and rotting leaves. I always liked that smell, when we helped Dad in the garden. He'd get John and me out to clean and bury the garden in the fall and turn soil each spring, a nice plot with tomatoes, beans, lettuce and peppers, carrots and cucumbers, always squash and sunflowers. Their house sits on an acre and a half, the garden along the back, blackberry bushes at one end. Gardening had been something that his father had taught him. It's funny that my grandparents came from Germany, with an accent that stays with Grandma to this day. Grandpa too, until he died before Laura and I got married. I once wrote to Laura that she didn't have to go all the way to Stockholm to marry a German. Grandpa said he came to America because he had been called into the army and decided it was time to seek his fortune elsewhere. He said he was a lover, not a fighter.

When Dad got drafted during Vietnam, Grandpa suggested he take a job with our cousin who owned a company in Sweden. Some coincidence, now that I think of it. Dad spent the better part of a year in East Asia, as he called it. He never talked specifics, but I met some guys he was in with. One had a glass eye, no thumb. I stubbed the cigarette out on the rock under me. I had to work at eight next morning, so I'd have to get home. But thinking about Pete made me reluctant to give up. I thought if anyone could find him, it would be me. This odd, thin kid in an oversized red jersey, number 13 on the back, and the long, wide black shorts, his mouth perpetually open on the field, watching intently as the ball and the striker ran past. No exaggeration, the absolute worst player I'd had in three years. When I looked, he'd be way off the sideline, paying zero attention, searching the grasses for crickets and hoppers. A couple of times he climbed a tree.

A guy like that sticks in the back of your mind. You're happy to forget about him but you can't, especially if he goes missing. Second half of our last game was a runaway. After our first and only goal, the Hillside Hawks took no prisoners. We took two guys off the field injured. In the last ten minutes I put in third stringers. When I looked for Pete, he was nowhere to be found. I asked a couple of kids where he had gotten to, and one of them pointed out a tree about fifteen feet off the sideline. Pete sat in the crotch smoking a cigarette. I ran over and yelled at him. I told him to put out the cigarette and get down if he wanted to go in. He looked down at me a moment and then leaned his head back on a branch. I was fit to be tied but had a game to finish, so I went back and got it over with. I had a pep talk with the boys about a good season and all of their best plays and so on, and the treat volunteer came over with health bars and Gatorade.

I left them sitting on the grass, talking and laughing amongst themselves, and headed to the tree Pete was climbing down. When I grabbed his shirt at the neck, his narrow shoulder stuck out. He looked so ridiculous with his floppy hair, big brown eyes and wet mouth. I set my hands on my hips, and he watched me staring at him. He looked so little and skinny, but I was pissed off about losing so badly. Pete represented the reasons we lost, so I shouted without thinking: "Jesus Christ, get your fucking head in the game."

When I went back to my team, I was still angry, complicated by how embarrassed I was I had said such a thing to the waif, which was how I thought of him. Time to send in the waif, I'd think before I called for Peter. I took them out for pizza, but Peter went home with his mother. I felt worse about this as the evening went on, until I had to let it go to get any sleep at all. I drank several brandies and prayed about it and corked off to sleep. That was on the weekend, and now here I was, sitting on a rock in the woods, ostensibly looking for Peter, thinking about my woes. I realized between game time and the present moment that I had related myself to Peter, because I felt I had been caught in a stasis myself, not an iota of change in my life, as if I was sitting in the tree with Peter smoking a cigarette.

No telling where he was, but it made me lonely thinking about him. I picked up a stick and snapped off twigs that ran along the main branch. I started thinking about Stockholm, about Laura with her German man and blonde boy named Hans. The pang that twisted in my stomach made me think I might be getting sick. I had not wanted a divorce at all was the main problem. I kept thinking she would come home soon, and we'd take up where we left off. She told me she didn't want to have kids for another ten years, maybe never, then she married Wolfgang and had Hans right away. If I didn't have the job and coaching, I couldn't have stood the emptiness. This Peter, this disengaged kid, caught up in isolation and disinterest, was missing. I had pretty much gone missing too, when Laura left. I should have quit my job, said good-bye to family, and gone with her, but that's not how I saw things. I would have been a tag-along husband. I had no idea what I would do. She'd have a job and be supporting us, and I would be doing what?

One of the things about being a young man is you need to be doing something, getting ahead, supporting your family. When I thought about Laura, I thought about the ocean between us. I felt the rocking of the waves until I got a hold on myself. If she needed me in an emergency, I couldn't get to her. But now she had Wolfgang. She wouldn't call me if she needed something urgently. I zipped my jacket because I'd started to feel the cold. I felt a drop of water on the back of my hand and wiped it off—trees dripping. I wiped the back of my hand on my pants. Someday it would come back, my mother said, with someone else.

But my emotions had hooked on this thorn in my past. Once the past backed away for another year or so, I could start over. I was pretty sure I wanted to join the church to have one more thing besides a job and coaching to occupy my emotions or spiritual yearnings, if that's what I had. If that had worked, I would have been grateful. I knew I could still answer the ninety-some questions, but I balked at asking my brother or sister to fill one out. My sister was mad at Laura for leaving. She tried to talk her out of it. She had two kids, boy and girl, and did not understand Laura's lack of interest in children. She became furious when she heard of Hans, calling Laura a liar. Though she had gotten over her anger, she could still tap into it when it came up. My brother John came to help out at soccer practice sometimes. I know he'd have said what I wanted him to say. I couldn't see a purpose to it now.

My parents would want to know why I couldn't stick to being Lutheran, like them. That ended when I met Laura—she ridiculed it into oblivion. I could no longer go back, but I maybe could claim something two thousand years old and steeped in ritual and anguish. But why in the world did I want to become Catholic if they didn't want me until I claimed everything before had been a mistake? The appeal was strong, the reaction just as powerful.

Of course, sometimes I thought there had been a flaw. Maybe the fact that Laura would take off and leave me like that indicated a flaw. When she finished the Master's Degree, she said her eyes had been opened. Her excitement rolled over all we had in Ohio. Nothing could stop her without creating resentment. I saw that clearly. I prayed every night that she wouldn't leave, and after she left, that she'd come back. I didn't get on my knees or anything. I lay in bed with my hands folded talking to God or someone I felt was listening. It went on a long time. Sometimes I moved my lips, as if I needed assurance of speech. I started praying about Laura first, and then touched on every member of my family before I got to myself, my feelings of loss and guilt and shame. Tonight, I would pray for Peter as well, my missing soccer player.

If I found him, if he materialized before me in the dark, I did not know what I would say to him. He was one of those boys who felt alone, though his mother loved him and wanted him back. His father lived in Cincinnati. I had already wondered if that's where he had gone, but his mother called there first thing. I realized not only didn't I know what I would say to him, I had nothing to say. I couldn't dispel his isolation, or his inadequacy for the life before him. He felt distant from his parents, the father who had moved away, the mother working to keep the house going. It would do no good to tell him they loved him. He would have to deal with that himself. Maybe someone else would know a way. I did not.

Pete, I would say, and that would be it. I might put my hand on his shoulder, and he would glance at it. He was an unattractive kid, prominent bones, overlarge eyes, a flat, lusterless brown that held no surprise or beauty. He did not know why he was here, what he was supposed to do, so he kept looking for the little things, bugs, leaves, sticks to swing at the grass. If he appeared in the woods, in the dark, stood before me and asked what I was doing here, what would I say?

"Coach, what are you doing here?"

"I was looking for you, Peter. The whole neighborhood came out to look for you."

"Where are they now?"

"They all went home, except for me."

If he asked for a cigarette, I would have given him one, and lit it. "Hey, buddy, you know that's not good for you. Stunt your growth, kill you eventually." He wouldn't even nod in acknowledgement. "Your mom is going to be upset when she learns where you've been."

He would look away, and that's when I would say what I had to say. "Look, I'm sorry I yelled at you. I'm not mad at you. It's not my right to be mad at you." But what I said, that still rang true. He had to get his head in the game. If he didn't, he would never do anything, never go anywhere. Of course, maybe he needed to get away from everything, to be himself for a while. I could understand that. I

187

cancelled myself out. Anything I thought to say, I thought of some other reason why I shouldn't say it. I was accomplishing nothing. It was time to go home, have a glass of brandy, read in bed a while. If I had found him, I would have walked him home to his mother, who would meet us at the door.

"Oh, thank God!" she would say. "Where did you find him?" She would throw her arms around him, hug him tightly.

"He was in the woods, Mrs. Johns," I would say. "Sitting in a tree. I saw him do things like that at practice and during games. I couldn't go in until I knew he was safe."

She would look at Peter as if just waiting to get him alone.

"What do you say to a boy like this, Mr. Miller?" she would say. Though it would not be a question, I would tell her I didn't know, which would have been the truth.

"Take care," I whispered, as I walked out of the woods. The moonlight became brighter. I crossed Cardinal and went between houses to Shaggy Birch Loop as it started, an early snow that would amount to nothing. It made me feel awkward, as if someone was watching in the dark. Or, maybe what I felt was no one watching me walk across neighborhood yards in a first snow, only a few windows lighted, shades pulled, curtains drawn against the night. I saw my own darkened house and went to it. I flipped on a light in the kitchen and stood with my hands on the counter. I knew Catherine would be upstairs in bed. She never stayed up past ten and just corked off like a baby. I saw myself pouring the brandy and taking it upstairs long before I actually poured brandy and went to bed.

Periwinkle slept on top of the covers, at the foot of the bed, and when I got in bed her tail thumped. I put my hand on her back to let her know I saw her. Catherine was breathing softly in sleep. She has a gift for sleeping, gentle as a child, the same way she lives her waking life. She's like a saint to me. If I could be more like her, I would be a happier man. I tend to brood, locked in my own dark thoughts. While I watched her sleeping, I thought about Peter, and then I closed my eyes and said a prayer for him. I remembered a Bible verse I memorized, at Peter's age, to repeat before my parents' church: Who among you, having a hundred sheep, if he loses just one, doesn't leave the ninety-nine in the wilderness and go after the lost one until he finds it?

That night I dreamed I saw Peter under a blue streetlight by himself, smoking a cigarette as he waited for a school bus that would carry him wherever he was going. He carried a net sack, such as we use for soccer balls, but filled with bones to mark the spot. I pulled over to offer him a ride, but woke in a dark room, Catherine and Periwinkle sound asleep, myself the only wakeful soul.

The next few nights, we met again to comb the neighborhood, up to the junior high and high school. We lost our energy for the search but persevered. For weeks and months, I kept a lookout for the missing boy, thinking that I caught a glimpse of him, a shadow drifting across the playing field. I feared our little patch of woods, though I strained my eyes to see inside whenever I drove by. A year had passed when we held a vigil, walking through the neighborhood with lit candles. He had become an idea we could not forget, as we waited for his bones to show the way to him.

# DRAGON

HENRY BONE, HIS wife Dolores, and their twelve-year-old son Isaiah lived in an impressive white colonial with three dormer windows at regular intervals along the roof. Below the roof, the balcony had been hung with loops of patriotic bunting. A dozen of Bone's key contributors, all of them town patriarchs, affectionately known as Bone-Heads, sat in state on the white wooden chairs, holding cool-looking drinks on the chair arms and china plates on their knees as they munched delicacies Chet Makens could only guess at from this distance.

Tucked under the balcony, a three-piece band ensconced on the porch played the familiar American tunes anyone in this midwestern town would recognize. At the moment, the guitarist, the banjo player, and a percussionist strumming a washboard with a thimble, banged out a tinny version of "If You Knew Suzie," all of them fairly shouting "O, o, o what a gal" on cue. In the side yard, ladies and gentlemen sat around a picnic table with a compliment of children chasing each other with wild abandon.

The enormous sign in the front yard announced *Hank Bone for Governor* in blue, a row of red stars beneath his name. Bone, proclaimed winner a week ago, had, in turn, begun a week of celebration, this final fete solely for his hometown. As dusk came, round paper lanterns hung about the house lit up, larger versions of the fireflies sparkling closer to the grass. Such a pretty scene, Chet reflected as he leaned against the green 1951 Buick Eight sedan he called The Dragon, parked at the curb halfway down the block, where he could watch the house through a gap in the boughs of a White Pine. He had bought The Dragon on orders of the voice, and for the same reason, more recently, contributed five hundred dollars to Hank's campaign at no small sacrifice, with a personal note to Henry, whom he had not seen in fifteen years.

Though he received no invitation for his trouble, he told himself, or the voice told him, that his substantial gift provided entry to the party under way at the Bone house. He had a hand-written note in the pocket of his jacket: *Chet, Old Friend, thank you so much for your generous donation, Hank Bone.* At the time Chet knew him, in high school, where he had been president of the senior class, and in Oklahoma City, where he worked for a newspaper, Henry had disliked the nickname *Hank,* but it had become part of the folksy appeal of his campaign. Cars came and went, some leaving, a few more pulling into the empty spaces. The favorite son had made good, so who knew what the future held?

Chet lit a cigarette, watching the progress of the night, sipping from a flask. Passers-by might have wondered why he leaned motionlessly by himself with so much going on around, but they could not know that he was never alone, a problem he hoped to solve coming here today. A rasping voice had been talking to him steadily since he was twelve years old, and he had learned to answer without moving his lips. Lately, he had grown eager to be rid of it, and the voice had at last agreed to terms of the negotiation. All he had to do was find a likely youth the same age as he had been, get close enough to him, and the transfer would be made. Young Isaiah filled the bill, and his connection to Hank made it seem like destiny.

The only thing that concerned him was meeting all of the articles of his negotiations with the voice, which had told him that the note in his pocket would give him entry to any party. The voice had been specific. To meet further demands of the oral contract into which he entered, he had purchased a pistol called the Hard-baller. Before he left Chicago, he took it to a range, firing several rounds to get the feel of the thing.

With four rounds remaining in the magazine, he speculated he would need one or two for the job. The voice reminded him what he had over Hank, a night sixteen years before. *You and Henry had good times back then*, the voice said.

191

We sure did, thought Chet—that brunette with the bright green eyes who called herself Cherry. One late night in Oklahoma City, Chet found Henry outside a bar, smoking a cigarette beneath a lamp post and hailed him as an old friend. This was back when Hank called himself Henry and worked for a newspaper. Chet had other reasons. He had made himself attractive to the law in his adopted city and was cooling his heels. In point of fact, the bombing of the federal building drew him there, where he was delighted to discover Henry Bone lived and worked.

Henry had not yet met the woman who would become his wife, so when Chet lay a hand on his shoulder and told him he looked thirsty, Henry slid right into the bar for a quick one that turned into a few. They ended the night at Chet's place, in the company of this brunette they had found in a condition of inebriation—Cherry—that made her susceptible to suggestion. They both had their share without protest until the sudden violence of exertions roused her enough that she threatened them with the law, something Chet wanted to avoid.

Henry slipped away before this became a nasty scene, leaving Chet to clean up for both of them. It could be, he supposed, that Henry did not know what precisely had transpired after he fled, but he certainly heard the girl's protestations. Though Chet had a pocket pistol at the time, he didn't want the noise. He got her to her feet, stark naked, and steered her down the hall to the bathroom, crying and complaining all the way.

Lifting her in his arms, he set her in the tub as gently as possible and dispatched her with a Ka-bar knife. She looked like a wild thing, green eyes wide open, her dark hair spread against the white tub, the red leaking from her throat and breast. He waited until she bled out and let the shower wash the blood away. Easily the hardest part had been dressing her again, dragging her down the stairs like an oversized doll, and driving her into the countryside, where he spent more than an hour digging a rectangular hole in a stand of quaking aspen.

He could not have accomplished any of this without the specific instructions of the voice that spoke continuously inside his head, right down to the copse of quaking aspens—for a sound they would make in the slightest breeze. He would never have thought to bring the required tools he had packed in the trunk. He took off his jacket and shirt, in order to preserve their cleanliness, and lay them carefully across his seat. He walked around to the back of the car, opened the trunk, and looked down at the assortment of tools, selecting the shovel, the spade, and the pick.

Slumped in the passenger seat, held up only by the seat belt, Cherry looked like she might be praying. With the encouragement of the voice, he chopped up the earth with the pick and dug without hurry or fear, piling excavated dirt in a heap beside the hole. Once it was deep enough, he pulled the car beside the gaping hole and tried to shove her into it by pushing with his shoes, on the instructions of the voice, hoping he wouldn't have to touch her again.

When she didn't budge, he heard a stream of recriminations, demanding that he release her seat belt. She fell forward, onto her knees, and when he gave a final thrust with his feet, she tumbled out head first. As he came around the car, he saw her lying on her back inside the hole, as if she was going to sleep for a very long time. He choked on of frenetic spasms of laughter which issued from his chest like sobs. As he covered her body with the first shovels of dirt, he told himself at least she would be warm. Before he spread earth over her face, he stood looking down at her, observing that she looked like a fairy princess.

*Finish the job, bury the drunken slut.*

Nevertheless, he knelt by the grave, and holding to the edge, leaned down and kissed her lips. He drew back, watching her face several minutes before resuming the task, ignoring the taunts and insults pouring into his mind. It took only a few minutes to finish the job. He patted the earth gently with the blade of the shovel. He brushed dirt from the tools before lining them up once more in the trunk, wiping his hands and forearms on a towel. He took his time donning the shirt and jacket once again before settling into the driver's seat.

Noticing her door remained open, he started the dragon, got out, and walked methodically around the car, avoiding the grave. He stared at the empty seat where her body had been, deeply moved. He was glad he had the time to give her the attention she deserved. With heavy heart, he slammed the door, a solid sound that reverberated in his mind as he slid back beneath the wheel and pulled onto the dirt road he took in.

When he got home, he showered, washing a stream of filth down the drain, drank a fifth of bourbon, and fell asleep on the couch. He had seen Henry several more times that year, but he did not relish spending time with Chet because of what transpired between them and the brunette with bright green eyes. He did not wish to speak of it, and thus he could continue to pretend not to know the fate of the girl Chet planted in a grove of quaking aspens.

In the meantime, Henry met Dolores, an Oklahoma girl, and got as far away as he could, back to his midwestern roots—the hometown where he and Chet grew up, while Chet went back to Chicago. When Henry and Dolores discovered they could not have children, they adopted Isaiah, who had grown to the same age Chet had been when he first heard the voice. It was for this twelve-year old boy the voice had brought him here. The handsome and charming Henry had become Hank, the councilman, then mayor, now governor-elect. Chet had come to collect what he saw as Henry's debt to him, even if it cost him five hundred bucks.

He had seen the boy in the paper, a skinny, dark-skinned lad just entering middle school. *Well, look at that*, the voice whispered. It had been thirty years that they had been together, Chet and his voice, and it seemed the voice too had tired of riding inside an aging host. In short, the voice promised to leave and enter this child if Chet could get close enough to make the transfer. Chet hoped the voice was not misleading him but did exactly as demanded. The burden had been so great the promise it would leave filled him with a hope he abandoned when it moved inside his head.

At the same time, he feared how it would be when he was free, without the voice to tell him what to do. Even so, he had moments when he doubted the voice had an identity separable from his own mind. At such moments, he heard the laughing and felt deeply ashamed. The voice was wise, and he was foolish. The first time Chet heard the voice, he had received a beating at the hands of his father and walked beside a stream near their home. His Dad had whipped him soundly for something he could not recall. The only thing he could recall was a recurring anger at his father, who led him to believe they were buddies until he turned on him with a smack to the head or a belt to his back and legs.

He picked up a stout stick he found along the way, pretending he had been beaten so hard he had developed a limp. When he heard a croak nearby, he spotted a green frog in the grass that hid it. Without further thought, he struck it with the stick, and the frog froze motionless. His deed shocked him so much he felt a rush of pity for the strange creature, but struck again, and kicked it back in the water, where it should have stayed.

It floated with legs spread in four directions. He heard a voice, distinct from anything he knew as himself, speaking in his mind, *Well, that's interesting*. If he had spoken, that might have been what he said, but he had not spoken. His shock at what he had done stilled his mind, and the voice penetrated the silence like a crack of lightening. He did not hear the voice for several days and wanted to hear it again, if only to validate that he had heard it the first time.

In order to call the voice, at last, he put his hands around the neck of the neighbor's calico and squeezed until it could neither yowl nor attempt to escape. When the lifeless cat lay between his knees, he heard the voice again. But then the cat stood, shook its head, and attempted to move away dizzily.

*Do you see the rock beside your foot?*

He froze, as the frog had, waiting to hear if the voice would speak again. *Bye-bye, kitty*, the voice whispered. Then soft laughter. The next time his father tried to strike, he grabbed his wrists and took him to his knees. The voice came from him, to the effect that if his father ever touched him again, he would make him sorry. When bone snapped, the man's face collapsed in pain and disbelief. A sense of power rushed into Chet's head. He said the word *Dad* with a sarcastic twist.

The moon put in an appearance, huge and red on the horizon, growing smaller as it slid up the sky, now yellow, now silver and shining. *Time to get on with it,* the voice told him, *unless you have chickened out.* The laugh followed. Chet stepped on the cigarette he dropped to the street and began walking toward the Bone house, where festivities were dwindling. His jacket was unnecessary on such a balmy night, but he had a weapon to hide. The trio were taking a break, each one competing with the other to see who could down more shots of tequila.

Chet told them to knock off, the party was over, and walked into the house. Evidently, he had not needed the donation extorted by the voice. The front door stood open. Several people—two men and a laughing woman—slouched in two white couches in the living room. Another woman lay sleeping on the floor, her head beneath a chair. A couple talked intimately in a sun room. He leaned in and told them it was time to go home.

"Oh," they both said, almost simultaneously. When he stepped back into the living room, he said, "Up and at 'm." He gave the woman on the floor a gentle kick to the soles of her feet. In no time he had the room cleared and moved to the kitchen, where he found Henry Bone leaning against the refrigerator laughing with two women who stood close to him.

"Clear out," he said to the women, "Mr. Bone and I need to talk."

Bone's long, handsome face grew angry at the interruption, but when he recognized Chet, his face drained of color, like the face of the woman in the tub. "Say, how have you been," Bone said, in a failed attempt at familiarity.

"I have a voice in my head, and I have to get rid of it."

"What are you talking about?"

"Listen, *Hank*, you know what I'm talking about. Remember the brunette with the bright green eyes? Cherry? You left before things got bitter. I had to ditch her myself. And, I do mean ditch. You've been pretending that didn't happen, am I right?"

"Is it money you want? Are you trying to shake me down?"

"I'm the guy who sent you five hundred bucks. If I wanted to shake you, you would be shaken." Chet took his elbow and ushered him into the dining room.

"What do you want?"

"Where is your wife?"

"What does it matter?"

"It matters—maybe she needs to know. Am I wrong?"

"We don't need to go there, brother," Hank whispered.

Though he resisted, Chet led him to the stairs. "I am not your brother," Chet said.

"What is it you want?"

"Your kid," Chet said. "Isaiah. Up we go."

"What are you talking about? You must be high."

"I'm high all right." On the landing, Chet reached inside his jacket, pulled out the hard-baller, and held the barrel against Bone's chest.

"What are you doing? I thought we were friends."

"I thought so too." Chet looked out the window, drawing Henry's attention. The crowd had cleared out for the most part. Tail lights pulled down the street. "Take me to her bedroom."

"Please, Chet, not this."

"Do it, my friend, or we will have it out right here."

When he wagged the pistol in his face, Henry said, "Down the hall, last door on the left. She's already in bed. For the love of God, Chet, let's stop this thing right here."

*Count it out,* the voice hissed. Chet set the barrel to Henry's forehead and said, "Count to three."

"We can work this out. I'll have a place for you at the statehouse, personal bodyguard. Top pay."

"I regret the hurry the situation requires, Henry. Would you like me to count it out for you?" He now felt relaxed, looking into the eyes of his old friend.

"For the...Dolly," he cried out. "Dolly, call the cops."

Without further fanfare, Chet pulled the trigger and the top of Henry's head exploded in red, spattering walls and ceiling, as well as Chet's face and hands. As Henry fell, Dolores came to her bedroom door—the near door, as it turned out—and leaned into the hall. She wore a white nightgown with tiny blue flowers, buttoned all the way to her throat.

"Get back in there," Chet ordered as he came at her.

She flailed, striking him in the face and arms so hard he dropped the pistol. It skittered across the hall and almost plunged into the stairwell. He slapped her face. She fell to the floor weeping, crouching away from him, holding her mouth. Chet dropped to his knees, took her neck between his hands. She tried to pull his fingers away, but Chet kept at it.

"Look, lady," he told her. "Dolly, is it? I'm fighting for my life, too."

Her face turned red and purple. Her eyes nearly popped from their sockets. Her tongue stuck out her open, red mouth. When she stopped struggling, her shoulders fell back.

Chet stood and went to the bedroom door, leaning on the jamb to catch his breath. When he saw a child staring at him, he hardly knew what it was: a frail, dark-complexioned boy, a bit taller than Chet expected, without a shirt. A wet spot grew on the front of his blue pajama pants.

*We're almost there. Make him stand still.*

"Stay calm," Chet said. "You're going to survive this thing." He took a step toward the boy, expecting something to happen. He had imagined this many times. "Stand where you are," Chet said. He looked down at his own chest, where the voice would exit to enter the boy. After a few minutes of standing close, he thought there should be a sign of the passage.

"Don't move," he told the boy.

When the boy dropped to his knees, he thought it might be happening, but he noticed the boy picking up the pistol he had dropped. He watched as the kid stood, pointing the barrel at his chest. His temple throbbed and his face burned.

*Think fast, idiot*, the voice said. Chet kicked at the boy, catching him under his hands. The pistol flew over his head and dropped behind him, rattling down the stairs. He pushed the boy against the railing and ran down the stairs, holding the bannister, two and three

198

steps at a time. When he got to it, he took the pistol in his hands and looked up the stairs at the boy who leaned over the railing, staring down at him.

"Stay where you are," Chet demanded.

He came back up the stairs as the boy ran to a bathroom at the end of the hall. Chet heard the lock snap and pushed his chest against the door, ordering the boy to do the same on the other side. "Do as I say and this will be over in a moment. Don't and I will shoot you right through the door," he explained.

He remained in this position several minutes before he heard the window opening in the bathroom. "Stay where you are," he shouted. He had to give the voice whatever time it needed to make the transfer. "I won't hurt you, if you do as I say."

By the silence inside the bathroom, he realized the boy might have gone out the window, so he slammed the door with the bottom of his shoe several times, until the wood cracked. When he could see inside, he knew the boy had fled. Blackness of night lay out the window hole.

Chet ran down the hall and down the stairs. He leaped off the porch and went to the side of the house, where he saw the boy on the ground. When he stood beside him, prodding his back with one foot, he realized the boy was not conscious. He turned and fled down the yard, hitting the picnic table, spinning over it. He lost the pistol and spent precious minutes searching in the dark. Once he found it, he ran down the street and jumped in his car, turning the key in the ignition before shutting the door.

As he spun into a U-turn, the door slammed shut. He looked in the rear-view mirror, half-expecting to see the boy behind him, arms and legs flying. Chet hit the gas, and the dragon sped off, jerking into second, sliding into third on the freeway on-ramp.

"You promised me," he cried. He heard only the soft laughter, like wind rushing past the windows, or the hum of the engine as he raced the spectres that had pursued him all his life.

CPSIA information can be obtained
at www.ICGtesting.com
Printed in the USA
LVHW022143280121
677615LV00012B/622

9 781716 449239